"Move your hand over just a little bit."

His hand settled on her belly and she had to remind herself to breathe. The baby kicked again. "There. Did you feel it?"

"Wynn," he said, his voice quiet. "It's a baby."

It was crazy and weird and somehow perfect, to have this little life growing inside her. She nodded. "Yeah, she's really there. Isn't that just the coolest thing?"

The look of wonder in his eyes nearly undid her. She took a couple of steps away and he tugged her back, scooping her into his arms again. "Break's over. Now you're going in the pond."

"What? No!" She gave him her sternest face. "Latham, you can't throw me in the pond."

"Oh, all right." He set her on the ground. "Come on, Mama, let's go paint your door."

She followed him onto the porch, heart slamming in her chest. *No, no, no, no.* It was not possible for her to be falling for Latham Grant again.

Not possible at all.

Award-winning author **Stephanie Dees** lives
in small-town Alabama with her pastor husband
and two youngest children. A Southern girl
through and through, she loves sweet tea,
SEC football, corn on the cob and air-conditioning.
For further information, please visit her website
at stephaniedees.com.

Books by Stephanie Dees

Love Inspired

Family Blessings

The Dad Next Door
A Baby for the Doctor
Their Secret Baby Bond

Their Secret
Baby Bond

Stephanie Dees

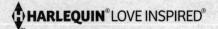
HARLEQUIN® LOVE INSPIRED®

Recycling programs
for this product may
not exist in your area.

LOVE INSPIRED BOOKS

ISBN-13: 978-1-335-42797-7

Their Secret Baby Bond

Copyright © 2018 by Stephanie Newton

All rights reserved. Except for use in any review, the reproduction
or utilization of this work in whole or in part in any form by any
electronic, mechanical or other means, now known or hereafter
invented, including xerography, photocopying and recording, or in
any information storage or retrieval system, is forbidden without
the written permission of the editorial office, Love Inspired Books,
195 Broadway, New York, NY 10007 U.S.A.

This is a work of fiction. Names, characters, places and incidents are
either the product of the author's imagination or are used fictitiously, and
any resemblance to actual persons, living or dead, business establishments,
events or locales is entirely coincidental.

This edition published by arrangement with Love Inspired Books.

® and TM are trademarks of Love Inspired Books, used under license.
Trademarks indicated with ® are registered in the United States Patent
and Trademark Office, the Canadian Intellectual Property Office and in
other countries.

www.Harlequin.com

Printed in U.S.A.

A man's heart deviseth his way:
but the Lord directeth his steps.
—*Proverbs* 16:9

To my family

Love is real and it looks a lot like you.

Acknowledgments

Many thanks to my amazing editor Melissa Endlich
and agent Melissa Jeglinski. Special thanks to
Sierra Donovan, critique partner, friend
and most patient person in history.

Chapter One

Wynn Sheehan unlocked the back door and stepped inside the dark storage room. In less than an hour, the quiet would be overwhelmed by clanging pots, sizzling bacon, coffeepots hissing and the murmur of simultaneous conversation. For now, though, she had the Hilltop Café all to herself.

She tucked her long blond hair into a knot and started the morning checklist. Open the blinds, turn on the lights, start the first pot of coffee and the first batch of cinnamon rolls, scramble the eggs, make the batter. She'd watched her mother go through these same motions, and there was something comforting about it. No matter where she had gone, or what she had done, things here, at least, stayed the same.

Measuring flour, shortening and buttermilk, she made the biscuits from a recipe she would've sworn she'd long ago banished from her memory. She'd had plans, a sackful of dreams to leave this little town and make her mark on history. She was going to change the world. She'd been passionate and driven.

And naive. So unbelievably naive.

Never would she have thought she would be back at the Hilltop, or back in Red Hill Springs, for that matter, but the Wynn who left for college with stars in her eyes, never planning to come back, was gone.

She'd found herself with no choices and worse, no friends. She didn't even know when it had happened, how she'd gotten so isolated. Well, looking back, she did know how. She'd been so focused on her job and her boss, the charismatic congressman from Virginia, that she hadn't had time for anyone else.

She hadn't even *seen* anyone else.

The timer dinged and she pulled the cinnamon rolls out of the oven, then slid the first pan of biscuits into place. Next up, the frosting for the cinnamon rolls.

By the time she got to the task of unlocking the doors, it had been an hour and a half. Six a.m. straight on the dot. And Mr. Haney and Mr. Donovan were waiting outside the door, just like they always were.

Mickey, the cook, let himself in the back door and made his way into the kitchen, lifting his apron off the hook and dropping it around his neck.

"Cutting it close, aren't you, Uncle Mickey?"

His bushy gray eyebrows lowered even farther over his eyes. "Where's your mother?"

"She's out at the farm helping Claire get the kids ready for school. Joe had an emergency callout in the middle of the night. Don't worry, I didn't mess anything up."

He slid his hand into a pot holder and pulled out the biscuits before sending her a sideways glance. "Never said you did, girlie. Now get out there and see what the customers want. Lanna doesn't come in until seven today."

Armed with a pot of coffee, Wynn rounded the counter with a smile for Mr. Haney and Mr. Donovan. "Hello there, gentlemen."

Mr. Haney looked up from squinting at the menu, his reading glasses tucked into the front pocket of his overalls, as usual. "Well, hello, darlin'. I'm going to be back here tomorrow if I get to look at that pretty face."

"You're here every day, Mr. Haney." Wynn sent him a wink, filled his mug and dropped a handful of creamers onto the table for her favorite farmer.

Mr. Donovan nodded to her as she poured his coffee. "I'll have the blueberry pancakes."

"Cinnamon roll and bacon on the side for me, Wynn." Mr. Haney slid his menu back into the holder. "I don't know why I look at the menu. I get the same thing every day."

"I'll keep the coffee coming." She turned back toward the counter and discovered that when she'd been in the kitchen with Mickey a couple more men had settled in a booth toward the front.

The practiced smile firmly in place, she started toward them, her feet stumbling to a stop as she realized one of them was her brother's friend Latham Grant. He'd practically grown up in the room next door to hers, and when they were teenagers she'd had the most miserable crush on him, one which left her stuttering over her words and tripping over nonexistent things.

They'd been friends, too, until they weren't. She closed her eyes for a brief second. There were so many things she needed to do here, so many relationships to repair. Nothing like returning home to give you some clarity about all the people you'd hurt along the way.

She hadn't seen him around in the month or so she'd been back. Maybe it was wishful thinking to have hoped it would stay that way.

He was just as ruggedly good-looking as he always had been, with muscles from actual work and not the gym, and that lock of dark hair that curled onto his forehead as he studied the menu.

She took a deep breath and stepped forward with a brisk smile. "Hey, Latham. Good to see you again."

He looked up, an easy grin on his face. "Wynn Sheehan. I heard you were back in town. Never thought I'd see the day."

When he stood to hug her, tears stung her eyes and she blinked them back with a pathetic attempt at a laugh. "Yeah, neither did I."

Those dark chocolate eyes, which had always been just a little too perceptive, narrowed in on hers.

She stepped away from him, away from the temptation to linger and rest her head on his broad shoulders, and turned to his grandfather. "Hey there, Mr. Grant. Coffee?"

"You know me too well." The twinkle in his gray eyes matched his grandson's. "Bertie, how is it that you never get a day older?"

She glanced at Latham, the smile on her face wavering a little bit. He shook his head just slightly.

"Good genes, I guess, Mr. Grant. You ready to order?"

He stuck the menu back in the top of the napkin holder. "I'll have my regular. You know just how I like it."

Latham cleared his throat. "We'll both have grits and biscuits with two eggs, over easy."

His grandpa scowled at him. "You don't like your eggs over easy."

"You're right, Pop. My mistake. I definitely want mine scrambled instead."

Wynn made a little note on the order sheet and shot them a smile. "Got it. I'll be back around with more coffee in a few minutes."

Wynn stuck the Grants' order into the wheel and spun it around for Uncle Mickey before grabbing the plates for Mr. Haney and Mr. Donovan. The bell on the door jingled, the first wave of the before-school crowd coming in.

The woman in the door, Wynn's friend Molly, had a baby drooling on one shoulder and her preschool daughter with a death grip on her hand.

"Oh, Wynn. Thank God. Here." She shoved the baby at Wynn and ran for the bathroom with the little girl.

"Molly, wai—" Wynn stared wide-eyed at the infant in her arms. The baby stared back, big blue eyes slowly filling with tears. Wynn started swaying. "Oh, no. No, you don't."

A loud wail followed the tears. She gave the infant, who was rapidly turning red, an awkward pat on the back. "Come on, baby, please don't cry. Your mama will be right back, I promise."

Latham appeared at her side, digging in the diaper bag and coming up with a pacifier. He popped it in the baby's mouth and she stopped crying, although she continued to stare accusingly at Wynn.

Latham laughed, a deep warm chuckle. "There you go."

Molly returned from the bathroom, blowing her bangs off her forehead. "Whew. Never let a potty-training three-year-old wear tights. Never."

Wynn's pulse raced, her breath catching in her throat. She pushed the baby back into Molly's arms and tore through the kitchen, pulling off her apron as she went. Lanna was in the office hanging up her purse. She looked up at Wynn, and the welcome on her face changed to concern. "You okay?"

"No. I've got to get out of here. You'll be okay?"

"Yes, go."

Wynn grabbed her keys off the hook and

slammed out the back door, falling back against it after it closed. She dragged air into her lungs, willing herself not to pass out.

Unwanted tears, nausea, panic attack. Lost career, lost love, lost nerve. She closed her eyes, her hands settling over her belly.

The person in high school voted "most likely to change the world" had come home in shame, and now? The only thing she'd be changing was diapers.

Latham unlocked the door of the sunroom from the outside, his two German shorthair pointers bumping up against his legs. "Okay, fellas, calm down. You got a lot of work to do today, Pop?"

"It's been kind of slow lately, but there's always some dusting to be done." His grandpa patted the newspaper under his arm. "I've always got the crossword if I get bored."

"Okay, then. Some boxes came for you and I stacked them by the door. I'm going to work, but I'll see you later."

His grandfather was already pulling open the boxes to unload the same cans he'd unloaded the day before. Every night after Pop was tucked into bed, Latham took a few cans off the shelves he'd made for the sunroom, and every day Pop restocked them. The small thing made Pop feel like he was doing something useful and made Latham feel like he was doing something—anything—to make Pop's quality of life just a little bit better.

Latham unlocked the door to the main house. The dogs tried to nose their way past him, and he nudged them back with his knee, an unnecessary act as a car in the driveway caught their full attention.

Pop's caregiver, Fran, slammed the car door shut and shooed the dogs back toward him. "Hooligans, the lot of you. Latham, you need to teach these boys some manners."

"Agreed," Latham said mildly. Fran was a whole lot of bluster. "If you'd quit feeding them treats all the time, they might leave you alone. Pop's in the sunroom, and I've just put a pot of coffee on for you. I'll be in the barn for a little while, and I've got a couple of small jobs today. Nothing else until I teach my class at the college at five. I'll have my cell phone on me if things change."

"I know the drill. I'll take him a cup of coffee and visit for a while."

As Fran entered the kitchen door, Latham headed in the opposite direction for the barn, the dogs at his heels. He'd tucked his work space into a grassy clearing at the back of the property, surrounded by pine trees. It wasn't unusual to come upon deer nibbling grass around the double-wide doors.

When both doors were wide open and the ceiling fans were on, he ran his hand down the reclaimed wood he was working.

The familiar earthy, pungent smell of the wood soothed his raw edges, the repetitive motions that created something out of nothing giving him a measure of peace for the things he couldn't control. He couldn't control Pop's illness, but he could control this.

He could shape and mold this wood into anything he wanted. This particular piece was turning into a beautiful farm table for some folks in the next county. In the barn, things happened at his whim and will.

He'd gotten Pop appointments with the best specialists in the Southeast, and there was no medical explanation for the elderly man's confusion, which started when Gran died unexpectedly. Nothing showed up on MRIs or CT scans.

It was as if Pop simply didn't want to live in a world without Gran. They'd been childhood sweethearts, married at sixteen, and had never been separated. They'd owned the local grocery store and gas station that anchored the town in a gentler, slower time.

Pop and Gran had been the only constant

in Latham's life when he was a kid. His parents weren't bad people, they just weren't settlers. They'd moved from place to place in search of, well, Latham wasn't sure exactly what they were in search of, but whatever it was, they hadn't found it yet. When he got old enough to understand the gift of a place to call home, he was grateful to them for leaving him in Red Hill Springs with his grandparents.

Because he was a settler. He liked his roots deep.

He leaned in, focusing on the task at hand, not looking up until he heard a car in the drive. He glanced at his watch. It wasn't unheard of for people to drop by out here, especially since Pop had come to live with him, but it was unusual.

Latham set aside his block of sandpaper and walked to the door of the barn. Wynn Sheehan got out of her car and slammed the door, looking around. For him, he guessed.

He grabbed a rag from the wood worktable beside the door, wiping the dust from his hands as he walked to the center of the clearing. This morning she'd had her hair tied back, but now, the whole long, blond length of it lifted in the wind.

He'd known she was home, of course—

the NSA had nothing on the gossip chain in Red Hill Springs, Alabama. He hadn't seen her, though, until this morning. She was as beautiful as she had been in high school when he'd been so awed by her, he couldn't put two words together in her presence.

She was opinionated and passionate and had a crazy understanding of the world and where she saw her place in it. He didn't know anyone else like her, and he'd wanted to be close to her, but she was his best friend's little sister and, as such, off-limits to the likes of him. They'd come close, once, to being more than friends, but even then he'd quickly come to understand that being rooted in this small town wouldn't be enough for her.

One hesitant step brought her closer to him, and her eyes locked with his.

Wynn broke the contact first, looking away as a mockingbird shot toward the sky, scolding them for being in the same space.

Latham met her at the edge of her car. "It really is good to see you, Wynn."

She smiled, but it didn't quite reach her eyes. "It's good to see you, too. It's been too long. I won't stay away that long again."

He wanted to ask her what kept her away, but they weren't really friends anymore. "What can I do for you?"

"My mom asked me to come and give you some pictures of what she's thinking about for the table she wants you to build for her. She could've texted them, but she insisted. You know Bertie."

"I do. There's no getting around her when she has her mind set on something. Come in. I was about to take a break. Want a Coke?"

"Water?"

He grinned. "I have that, too."

"I didn't even know that you were handy with a saw in high school."

"I could've probably made a birdhouse in high school, but it wouldn't have been pretty." He looked up from the small fridge in his office—a stall with a desk made from two sawhorses and some old boards. It suited him, though.

He handed her a small bottle of water. "I didn't start seriously working with wood until about six years ago. I moved back here to be with Pop after Gran died. I do some carpentry work and odd jobs, but there's just not that much to do in Red Hill Springs. I needed a hobby, desperately."

"So you just decided to build something?" She was wandering from photo to photo, which he had meticulously hung on the wall.

Every item he ever built, starting with the first wooden box, was represented there.

"Yeah, I found some plans for a porch swing online and decided to make it. Back then, I had to get the lumber store to do all my cuts for me." He waved a hand at the huge saw in the back of his shop. "Now I use mostly reclaimed wood and I do everything here."

She ran a finger down the table he'd been working on this morning. "Beautiful. You're really talented. It's a kind of art."

Surprised, he searched out her face. "It is, in a way. I remember you being the artist, though." He glanced at his watch. He needed to leave soon so he could get his jobs done and be at the college before five. "So Bertie sent you out here with some photos?"

She handed them to him and smiled, the first real smile he'd seen from her all day. "I think it was a ploy to get me out from under her feet. I'm not used to being at home, but Bertie isn't used to me being home either."

His hands, smoothing the thin magazine sheets, stilled, and he asked the question he'd been wanting to know the answer to since he first heard she was back in town. "Are you planning to stick around for a while?"

The smile vanished. "I'm not sure. I'm still

trying to figure all that out. I better go. Tell your pop I said hi."

He followed her to her car. "You're welcome to stay and tell him yourself. I teach a class at the college, so I've got to get going or I'd go in with you."

When she opened the door, he reached for her hand. She stared at it. "It really is good to see you again, Wynn."

She looked down where their two hands joined and didn't move for a long second. She swallowed hard. "I have to go."

"Take care." He watched as she drove away, his eyes following her little blue car until it disappeared around a curve.

He didn't wonder that he was still as fascinated by her as he had been as a teenager, just accepted it as a fact. That was his nature. But he did wonder what brought her back to Red Hill Springs and what it was that made her eyes look so sad.

Chapter Two

Wynn lay on the floor in her brother Ash's house, building a block tower with three-year-old Levi, whose adoption would be final in a couple of weeks. He was babbling constantly now, words mixed with sounds that had some resemblance to words.

There'd been a time, not that long ago, when they wondered if he would ever speak, or stand. He'd been broken, physically and emotionally, when Ash's wife, Jordan, became his foster mom. Together, Jordan and Ash had patiently helped him become a healthy, happy toddler.

When he pulled up to standing using the coffee table, she had to dive to save her glass of ice water from his busy fingers. "Guys, he's really doing so well."

Ash turned from where he was finishing

the spaghetti sauce on the stove. "He took two steps yesterday."

"What? With no hands? Levi, you big boy! Aunt Wynn is so proud!"

Levi let go of the coffee table and clapped his hands, delight shining in his dark brown eyes. Out of the crew of foster kids at Red Hill Farm, he was the first she'd bonded with, maybe because she felt wounded, as well. Her wounds were just on the inside.

Her brother turned a speculative blue gaze on her. "I heard you were out at Latham's today. You know, he had a crush on you in high school. He thought we didn't know, but it was so obvious."

Wynn opened her mouth and closed it again.

"Ash, don't forget the bread!" Jordan winked at Wynn as she poured the noodles into a colander and served them into bowls.

Ash pulled out a pan of perfectly toasted garlic bread and grinned at his wife. "Last time we had spaghetti, someone-who-shall-remain-nameless-but-wasn't-me forgot the bread was in the oven and the entire house filled with black smoke. So the fire alarm is going off, the baby's crying, Jordan's screaming that the new house is going to burn down. It was awesome."

"Ashley Sheehan, you don't have to tell all the family secrets."

His grin turned wicked. "Oh, don't worry, I won't tell her about the time you—"

"Ash!" Jordan dove across the kitchen to smash her lips against his, presumably to keep him quiet.

He came up laughing. "Okay, okay, I give."

"I thought so." A satisfied look on her face, Jordan picked Levi up from the floor and tucked him into his high chair. "Let's eat. I'm starving."

"You guys are nuts." Wynn stood, sliding her feet back into her short suede boots. "But the spaghetti smells delicious."

They were nuts in the best possible way. The little glances, the subtle—or not-so-subtle—innuendos, all hinted at a content life, a happy marriage, something Wynn wasn't sure she would ever have. Not now.

She'd let herself be blinded by her boss's shine and bigger-than-life persona, somehow convincing herself that her place was behind the man, supporting him in his bid to change the world. He'd encouraged that, cultivated it, made her think she was indispensable to him as the love of his life.

She'd believed him.

She'd even believed him when he told her

he wasn't ready for marriage, that his work as a congressman had to come first. That is, until she'd seen the piece about his engagement in a political blog with impeccable sources.

Her world had fallen out from under her. Preston was getting married—just not to her. When she'd discovered her pregnancy a month later, he accused her of sleeping around and trying to trap him into marrying her.

She hadn't spoken to him since.

When she looked up, her brother's perceptive eyes were on her face. She forced a smile and took a huge bite of spaghetti that she wasn't sure she could swallow.

Jordan laid her fork down. "So, Wynn. Everyone is wondering why you're home and how long you're planning to stay."

The instant wave of nausea dispelled any appetite that Wynn may have started out with. Apparently, all of Red Hill Springs had decided that they'd given her enough space and it was time for answers.

Deliberately, she picked up her glass of ice water and took a drink. She cleared her throat. "To be honest, I'm not really sure. *Indefinitely* seems to be the most accurate answer."

Ash's handsome face softened. "Wynn, are you okay?"

She pressed her fingers into her temples, where a headache had begun to throb, and took a deep breath before looking her brother in the eyes. "I'm fine. But… I'm probably going to need the services of the family pediatrician in about six months."

"You're pregnant?" Her new sister-in-law squealed and jumped up from her spot at the table to give Wynn a hug. "Why didn't you say anything?"

Wynn held on to Jordan just a little too long. She hadn't expected happiness. She'd expected pointed looks, maybe some outright condemnation, a judgmental whisper or two. "I messed up. And it's a pretty obvious mistake, or, at least, it's going to be."

Jordan flopped back into the chair, her auburn braids bouncing on her shoulders. "You've put the mistake behind you. You're here, aren't you?"

Wynn searched out her brother's gaze. He was quiet. Too quiet. He shook his head, and her stomach plummeted again.

But then he said, "Jordan's right, Wynn. Maybe you made some bad choices, but no matter what happened to get you to this point, a baby is a blessing, not a mistake, and we're going to love him."

"Or her." A tear dripped down her cheek, and she mopped it with her napkin. "I never used to cry."

Jordan grinned. "Me either. I don't even have pregnancy hormones to blame, but I cry all the time now."

"Have you told Mom?"

"Not yet." At her brother's look, Wynn grimaced. "I know, I know. I will. It's just—it's Mom. I don't know, Ash."

"You have to tell her. It'll only get worse if you don't. Are you going to stay there?"

"For now, but if I stay in Red Hill Springs—"

"You should. You totally should." Jordan interjected her opinion with a firm nod. "You need family around when you have a baby. Trust me on this one."

"If I stay in Red Hill Springs," Wynn continued, "I have to find a job and a place to live."

Ash and Jordan exchanged a look.

"What?"

Jordan tore another piece of toast in half and slid it onto the tray of Levi's high chair. "I don't know about the job, but Claire and I were planning to offer you the cottage at Red

Hill Farm, even before this. It really would be perfect for you. And Claire and Joe would be right there."

Wynn's other brother, Joe, was married to Jordan's twin sister and, together, they had somewhere around ten kids. The number was always changing as foster kids came in and out of their home, but they'd made Red Hill Farm into a peaceful place to heal.

Wynn hadn't even considered the cottage. "I thought I heard you and Claire were converting the cabin to office space."

"We were." Levi threw a handful of spaghetti across the table and Jordan whisked his plate away. "Okay, we're done with spaghetti and Daddy needs a clean shirt."

Jordan gently disentangled one of her braids from Levi's sauce-covered fingers. "Gross, Levi. So yeah, we were planning to convert the cottage to office space, but honestly, I do most of the office work at home now because it's more convenient and Claire doesn't have time to make use of a separate office."

Ash gave up wiping spaghetti sauce off his formerly pristine white shirt and leaned back in his chair. "You know, everyone who lives in that house falls in love."

Wynn rolled her eyes. "Thanks for pointing that out to your pregnant sister, who has, in fact, sworn off men forever. I don't think you have to worry about me falling in love with anyone."

He took a sip of his iced tea and raised one eyebrow. "Whatever you say."

"I say yes. To the cottage." She raised her voice. "Thank you, Jordan. The cottage will be perfect."

Jordan popped her head out from the bathroom down the hall, where water was running into the tub. "I have no idea what you just said, but I'm assuming from your smile that it was yes?"

Wynn nodded.

"Feel free to paint or whatever. It was a slap job when Joe renovated. I always meant to work on it and didn't get to do very much." Jordan disappeared into the bathroom again.

Wynn took the dishes to the sink. Her brother nudged her away. "I got this. Go home. You started work at four thirty this morning, and you have circles under your eyes."

She hugged her brother. "Thank you for dinner. And for...everything."

"You're gonna be fine, Wynn. You're the most courageous person I know."

Eyes swimming with tears again, she gave him a shove. "You're okay, yourself."

"Tell Mom."

"I will. Don't push me." She heard her brother's laugh as she swung down the stairs and opened the door to her car. So it looked like her "indefinite" stay here was getting a little more defined. By making that choice, she was deciding to face the scrutiny and reaction of people who'd known her all her life…people she respected and cared about.

Tomorrow, she would tell her mom. It wouldn't be easy. But already, she knew her brother had her back, and that was no small thing.

As she drove home, her brain was spinning with ideas for fixing up the cottage that she would soon be calling home, the realization that she was going to need help…and that Latham just happened to be a carpenter.

Latham pushed the door open to the bakery, stopping short when he saw Wynn sitting on a stool behind the counter, dressed in a long white T-shirt, black leggings and her sister Jules's signature pink apron. "I didn't know you were working here."

She smiled, a little sheepishly. "Apparently everyone in the family has been waiting for me to settle in so they could take a day off. So, yesterday at the Hilltop, today at the bakery."

He raised an eyebrow. "You bake?"

"Ha! No worries, Jules did all that before daylight. I'm strictly counter help. Where's Pop today?"

"He likes to meet his friends for breakfast at the Hilltop on Saturday morning, so I usually drop him off and come next door for one or two of your sister's cinnamon twist doughnuts. Which may or may not be why I have to play soccer with the guys on Saturday afternoons."

She laughed as she placed two cinnamon twists on a paper plate. "Yes, well, food is my family's love language, so I understand the need for exercise. Coffee?"

"Yes, please."

Wynn poured his coffee into a mug with the Take the Cake logo and handed it over the counter, accepting the cash Latham handed back to her.

"Join me? Please?" Latham pulled the other chair out and laughed when Wynn looked behind her like he might be talking to someone else. Her cheeks were pink, her straight blond hair looped into a half ponytail, half-bun thing.

She caught her bottom lip between her teeth as she considered, then grabbed the last of the cinnamon twist doughnuts and a napkin with a sigh. "I can't believe that I'm about to eat this. I never ate like this in DC."

"What did you eat?"

"Coffee, mostly. Takeout with the other staffers when we would work late, which was always."

"Why did you leave?" When she glanced up with an almost panicked look in her eyes, he wished he could take back the question. "I guess, I mean, I thought it was a perfect job for you. I'm sorry. I shouldn't have asked."

"It's okay, Latham. It's a perfectly normal question to ask. It's just…complicated. The short answer is that I changed, and I didn't like the changes."

His fingers itched to reach for her hand, slide her fingers into his. He didn't even know why—he certainly had no right to. He wrapped them around the warm coffee mug instead. "Sometimes coming home is the bravest thing you can do."

Her blue eyes flicked to his and held, and for a moment he thought she was about to say something. But then, the door opened, bells jingling. Wynn jumped to her feet and rounded the corner to greet new customers behind the counter.

He heard the murmur of conversation, registered kids jumping up and down at the prospect of a doughnut, but his eyes were on only Wynn. Would it be so weird for them to resurrect their friendship after all these years?

The boisterous family blew out as quickly as they'd come in. Wynn took a second to wipe the fingerprints off the glass and sat down beside him again, the friendly but distant smile firmly back in place. The moment of sharing whatever it had been was over. Which suited him because, honestly, it was a little embarrassing that he hadn't gotten over his adolescent crush sometime in the last ten years. No wonder the barn cats were his best companions.

He finished off the second doughnut, which he'd intended to save for this afternoon, and took a swig from his mug. "So are you going to be filling in for your family members often?"

Wynn laughed. "Mercy, I hope not. I don't know what I'm going to do, though."

Latham took a breath and then thought, what could it hurt, since he'd already taken the awkward quotient through the roof? "Would you be interested in staying with Pop in the afternoons for a couple of weeks? His current caregiver had a family emergency."

She blinked, and heat rushed his face. "I know it's way below your pay grade... I shouldn't even ask."

"I'd love to."

He narrowed his eyes. "No, you wouldn't."

"I really would, Latham. Your home is beautiful, and Pop is great. I think I'd like spending time with him."

"Me, too, but..."

"Really, it's my pleasure. I do have one request, though." There was a suspicious gleam in her eye that made him laugh as she leaned in.

"Name it."

"In lieu of payment, can we work out a trade?"

Latham relaxed back into his chair. "I'm a little scared of that look in your eye. What did you have in mind?"

She grinned. "I'm moving into the cottage at Red Hill Farm, which needs some work. I propose that I get to enjoy conversations with Pop in the afternoon and you help me with the cottage when you have time."

"You've got a deal." How much could she want to do at the cottage? It was only eight hundred square feet, tops. Either way, it worked out. He really needed someone at his place in the afternoons, and if he helped her with the cottage, he would get to spend time with her.

Win-win.

"You know, I totally got the better end of the deal here. I get to spend afternoons with Pop, which I will love, and I get free labor on the reno. Win-win for me." She laughed, and her eyes, for the first time since he'd seen her, were shining.

And he knew in that second that he would've done anything she asked, just to make her smile. "If your family doesn't have plans for you, I could meet you out there after church tomorrow and look it over."

"Bring Pop to family lunch at the farm and we can check it out after we eat."

"I'm gonna end up holding a couple of kids while they smear peanut butter on me, aren't I?"

"I see you've been to family lunch before." She grinned. "I feel like we should shake on it. I'm pretty sure you're going to regret this deal."

He laughed and took one last swig of his coffee as he stood. "Not a chance. I'll see you tomorrow afternoon."

But he took her outstretched hand, his eyes

on hers. He swallowed hard when her eyes widened at the contact. She pulled away, busying herself clearing the table, and he sighed.

He may regret this deal, but not for the reasons she thought. He'd spent a long time getting over her when she left Red Hill Springs. He just hoped he could keep the past in the past where it belonged.

Chapter Three

Wynn stood outside the attic door in her mom's house. She'd been walking past it for weeks now, staring at the doorknob, wanting to go in, but not wanting to, just as much.

She shook her head at herself as her hand lingered over the knob. Who was this woman who didn't have the courage to walk through a door? What happened to the little girl who punched a kid at Vacation Bible School because he was being a bully? Where was the little girl who believed in justice, even if it meant she'd be in timeout for the rest of the afternoon?

That little girl would have the courage to open a door. It was just a door.

She turned the knob and shoved it open, blinking at the swirl of dust in the warm air. Her studio had been the place she'd gone to, as a teenager, when things got rough or rocky. Or sad or happy or confusing.

Her mom hadn't changed much, if anything, in the tiny room tucked into the eaves of the old house. Wynn's paints were still haphazardly strewn on the desk and her easel held a small unfinished watercolor. She picked up the sketchbook from the top of a teetering stack of identical books. When had she lost the wonder she'd always had at the world around her?

Probably around the same time she stopped looking at her job as an opportunity to make things better for someone else and started looking at it as a career. She'd lost her ability to dream, to think of others besides herself. Worse, she'd lost her confidence in herself and her faith that God had a plan and kept His promises.

Somewhere along the way, she'd imagined that her plan was better.

Well, she could see how that turned out.

She'd like to blame Preston. And while he definitely shared the blame, it wasn't all his fault. She was the one who'd let go of her morals and her beliefs. She was the one who replaced her dreams with his—until he replaced her in his life with the newer, prettier, more idealistic model.

Wynn slid her hand down around the very small, almost imperceptible curve of her belly, and whispered, "I promise I'll do better."

She had to. She had barely six months to figure out how.

The room was dusty, the paper she had painted on dry and curling at the edges. The whole space looked used up and ready for the trash bin. Fitting. That's exactly how she felt.

Sweeping the pile of dried-up paints into the trash can, she tried to imagine that she was sweeping out the parts of her that she didn't want anymore, the parts that didn't work for her and could never be salvaged. Maybe it all just needed to go.

She caught her breath on a sob.

The watercolor paints—those she could keep. They were dried up and cracking with disuse but…they could be revived with a little tending.

Maybe the vibrant parts of her, the passionate, giving part of her, could be revived with a little tending. She would start by carrying her sketchbook and pencil in her bag again. For a long time, that sketchbook had served as a place for her to record her impressions, ideas and dreams.

Yes, her soul needed tending. The favorite

part of what made her who she was had been sadly neglected.

The worst part is that if anyone had asked her as a high school senior if she would ever let a man get in the way of her priorities, she would've been so offended.

A slight knock sounded at the doorway to the small studio. Wynn scrubbed the tears from her cheeks. When she turned, her mom was standing in the opening.

"Hey. I wondered when you would come in here."

"It's been too long. Mom, I don't know why I didn't come home more."

"You were busy trying to find out who you were."

Wynn laughed, but the sound wasn't cheerful. "It's funny, but I think I had to come home to find out who I really am. I keep saying I don't know how I got to this point, but I do. I let a man come between me and what I knew was right. I let my desire to make a difference somehow become a desire to be wanted and needed. And he was only too willing to take advantage of it."

Bertie walked closer and studied the painting on the easel. "He…the congressman?"

"Preston Schofield the fourth, career politician." She pressed her lips together in a firm line.

"You seem a little bitter, Wynn. Congressman Schofield gave you a great opportunity."

Once, Wynn had believed that to be true. Now she knew better. "Mom, I'm pregnant."

"Oh, honey." Bertie's face softened in sympathy, but she didn't look shocked.

Wynn sucked in a breath and, unable to meet her mother's eyes, whirled around to look out the window. "You aren't surprised. How long have you known?"

"I didn't know who—but I've known you were pregnant since just after you got home. I'm your mom, Wynn. Did you think I wouldn't guess?"

Wynn's eyes filled with tears, the familiar walls of her studio blurring as words she'd been longing to say came pouring out. "I'm sorry. I wanted to tell you. I just didn't…want you to be disappointed in me."

Her mom turned Wynn to face her, wrapping her arms around her as she did when Wynn was a child. "I'm not disappointed in you, Wynn. Everyone loses their way once in a while. I used to tell you when you were little that nothing you could do would ever make me stop loving you. It's still true."

Wynn took a deep breath and released it,

along with some of the tension knotting the muscles in her back. "I don't know what I'm going to do yet. Claire and Jordan offered me the cottage."

"That's a good thought." Her mom picked up one of the small paintings and studied it. "I've been meaning to clean out in here for years. Why don't you start by remembering who you were before all this happened?"

A phone rang from somewhere in the house. Bertie put the painting on top of another pile of things. "I've got to get that, and then I'm going to make a chocolate cake. Come down to the kitchen when you're ready for a break."

Wynn glanced at her watch. "I actually have to go. I promised Latham I'd stay with his pop this afternoon. I won't be late, though."

"No problem. Chocolate cake will keep."

"I love you, Mom."

Already halfway out the door, Bertie turned back. "I love you, too, baby girl. And I just can't wait to see what God has in store for you next."

As her mom disappeared down the hall, Wynn heard the muffled hello as Bertie answered the phone. She turned back to her studio, the room where she'd dreamed and planned and painted. Soon the smell of her favorite chocolate cake would be in every nook and cranny of the house. Each one of Bertie's kids had their favorite comfort food. For Wynn, it was always chocolate cake. Jules loved bread; Ash, cinnamon rolls; and Joe, chocolate chip cookies. Bertie would bake, and then they would sit at the table with a glass of milk and talk it out.

She stood in the door to the studio, her hand on the knob. Deliberately, she walked away, leaving it open.

Downstairs, she picked up her keys from the counter in the kitchen. Bertie was unloading ingredients from the pantry to the counter. "Mom, Mr. Grant thought I was you when I was filling in at the Hilltop. Does he have some kind of dementia?"

"Something like that, from what I understand. I don't know the details, but he's really gone downhill since Mrs. Margenia died a couple of years ago. I'm driving car pool for Claire this afternoon, but I could come out after I get the kids to the farm."

"No, thanks. I'm sure I'll be fine."

In the car, on the way to Latham's place, Wynn's stomach tumbled with nerves, but she had no reason to be anxious. This wasn't rocket science. This was being kind to someone who needed help.

She might've been in Washington, DC, a long time, but she still remembered how to be kind.

Latham pushed the back door open silently. He'd gotten called in to sub in one of the freshmen history classes and was an hour later getting home than he'd planned on being.

The house was quiet, the TV murmuring in the background. Wynn sat at the kitchen table, late-afternoon light creating a halo around her hair as she sketched on a pad. She was so pretty. Always had been, but in high school it hadn't been her looks that drew him to her.

It had been her absolute fearlessness.

He'd known then she was different from other girls, but now that he spent his evenings teaching college students, he was even more aware how rare that kind of self-confidence was. He dropped his backpack and she looked up, a smile in her eyes.

"I'm sorry. I was late and you spent your whole afternoon here." Latham glanced over at Pop, napping in the recliner in the living room, a glass of iced tea at his fingertips on the side table. "He's been okay?"

"Aside from being a little confused that Fran had to leave and I was here, he's been totally fine. I hope it's okay that I raided the garden to cook his supper."

He shot her a grin and relaxed. "Feel free to raid my garden anytime, especially if you're going to cook in my kitchen. Are those fried green tomatoes?"

"Yes. Your grandpa really liked them."

"They're his favorite and I always make them too soggy." Latham popped one in his mouth. Even cold, it was delicious.

"The key is the ratio of cornmeal to flour. I'll email you the recipe, if you promise not to tell Bertie. Trade secrets and all." Wynn stood and grabbed her sketch pad. "I should probably be going."

"Join me for some tea on the back porch?" The words were out and hanging in the air before he even knew he was going to say them.

Her eyes, glass blue and crystal clear, met his, and he could see her hesitation. "Please? I could use some adult conversation after the class I just taught."

She nodded. "So, no one cut their finger off today?"

Confused, he looked up from pouring tumblers of sweet tea. "No, you mean like with a saw?"

"Isn't that what you do in shop class?" She held the back door open for him to walk through.

He laughed and handed her a drink as they sat down. "I teach Government, although I was filling in for World History this evening."

Her cheeks tinged with pink. "I'm sorry, I just assumed you'd be teaching carpentry."

"You wouldn't be the first. I have a Master's degree in Political Science, so naturally I build things for a living. Makes sense, right?"

"Hopefully you're building good citizens as well as beautiful tables."

He clinked his cup to hers. "That's the idea. Hey, you should come and speak to my class some time."

"Me?" Her expression was shocked and just a little horrified. "Why?"

"Most of them have probably never met anyone who worked on Capitol Hill. You could give them some insider info, what it's really like."

Her face shuttered. She set the glass on the small table beside her chair. "I don't think so. Listen, I have to run. I promised my mom I'd be home for dinner tonight."

Latham got to his feet, aware he'd said

something to upset her but not sure exactly what it was. "Sure thing."

He walked her to the car and opened the door for her. "I can't tell you how much I appreciate you staying with Pop. He's really special to me."

"I enjoyed it. And I'm looking forward to seeing him again tomorrow. Just let me know what time you need me." She slid into the driver's seat, and before he could say anything else, she was driving down his gravel drive toward the highway.

He shoved his hands into his pockets and watched her taillights fade into the distance. The door opened behind him and Pop stepped out onto the porch.

"Hey, old man. I thought you were out for the night."

Pop settled in a rocker, hanging his cane over the arm of the chair. "I was faking."

A laugh burst out. Latham stared at his grandfather. "What are you talking about?"

"Well, it's not like you bring pretty girls out here all the time. And you can't have meaningful conversation with your old grandpa butting in, now, can you?"

Latham shook his head. "Sometimes I have to wonder which one of us is more with it, Pop."

His grandfather, who had raised him from the time he was a toddler, chuckled to himself. "So, did you ask her on a date?"

Latham stared at the dusky sky, where the North Star was just beginning to glimmer. "No. I don't think she's interested in me like that. I couldn't even get her to agree to speak to my class."

"Your gran wouldn't go out with me when I first asked her. She had her cap set for that moon-face jerk Phillip Stewart. I was persistent, though. I asked her so often that I finally wore her down. She went out with me just to shut me up." Pop grinned, his laugh nearly a cackle. "That was the last time she mentioned Phillip Stewart."

Latham laughed. "The rest is history, as they say. Gran knew a keeper when she saw him. She was a smart lady."

Pop's eyes clouded. "Margenia?"

The lucid moment was gone. Latham tried to be grateful for it and not sad that it was over. As he held his grandfather's elbow and helped him into the house, his mind drifted to Wynn. She had come to his rescue with Pop when she didn't have to, but she sure didn't seem interested in spending any more time with him.

Pop recommended persistence. It had certainly paid off for him. Latham smiled.

Maybe he would have to give it a try.

The next Sunday, Wynn sat in a rocking chair under the big oak tree at Red Hill Farm, a two-month-old baby girl, the newest of Claire and Joe's foster children, in her arms.

This baby was small. Really small. How much smaller was a baby when it was a newborn? That terrifying thought speared through her mind as the baby met her eyes with a serious stare.

Family lunch had been the usual insanity. Kids running everywhere. Adults trying to snag a bite or two of food in between chasing the kids. Today two adoptive families had joined the fray, including the family who'd adopted ten-year-old twins, Jamie and John.

Claire dropped into the chair beside Wynn and handed her a lukewarm bottle. "I was on my way to get this when I heard screaming about blood gushing. Matthew cracked his knee open."

Wynn stuck the nipple in the baby's mouth. She'd given Ash and Jordan's little boy a bottle lots of times. It was no big deal. So why was sweat beading on her forehead?

The baby attacked the food with ferocity.

She seemed to know what to do. Wynn relaxed back in the chair, letting out a slow relieved breath. "So was there?"

Claire was staring into the distance. "Was there what?"

"Blood gushing?"

Her sister-in-law grinned, one hand pressing into her back, the other sliding around to rub her very pregnant belly. "Oh, yeah. Everywhere. Luckily, from experience, Ash knew to bring his medical kit to lunch today and he was able to super-glue the cut. No stitches unless Matthew breaks it open again. Which, let's face it, has a high probability of happening. That kid runs everywhere."

Latham came loping across the yard in front of them, his hands in the air, a football dropping into them. He was dressed in jeans, a faded red RHS T-shirt and his work boots. He tossed the ball back and held his hands up in surrender. "Dude, I'm old. I gotta rest."

He fell against the tree beside Wynn. "I really have to work out more."

Claire laughed. "I've been telling myself that for months. No one tells you that raising children is an extreme sport."

Latham peeked over Wynn's shoulder. "This one's new?"

"Yep, she's just here for respite, though. She goes back to her foster family next week."

"Cool. Pop's with a neighbor, but he'll be back pretty soon. Do you mind if I look at the cottage now?"

Surprisingly, the idea of giving up the sweet weight of the baby girl in her arms wasn't as welcome as Wynn had imagined it would be. She glanced at Claire.

"I've got her. Y'all go." Claire leaned forward and scooped the baby into her arms. "The cottage isn't locked."

Wynn fell into step beside Latham as he rounded the barn and skirted the edge of the pond. "I hope you're not going to regret this."

He placed a hand on her back as the path got a little unsteady. "Nah. Tell me what you have in mind."

"I want to paint the whole thing white, for starters. I love that Joe painted such crazy colors for his twelve-year-old daughter, but I'm a little too old for neon green and shocking pink."

His deep laugh rolled over her. "I can see that. So far, I'm thinking we could knock this out in an afternoon."

She glanced over at him as they stepped onto the porch. The little cottage was shabby, but despite that, it had charm. "I want the outside to be painted."

He studied it, stepped forward and knocked on the outside. "Might be better to replace this worn siding and insulate the walls. It would definitely help with your climate control."

"That's a great idea. Now for the inside. Most of the house just needs to be painted. I even love the rustic brick fireplace. But I need a studio. What do you think about opening up the attic space above the kitchen for a loft area?"

Latham scratched his head. "I mean, it could be done, no doubt. I'm guessing that's where the majority of your HVAC and plumbing is."

"But…"

He shrugged. "Where there's a will, there's a way, my granny used to always say. Let me nose around some and I'll get back with you on that."

Wynn threw her arms around his neck. "I knew you could do it."

He gave her an awkward pat on the back, his cheeks red when she stepped away from him. "Don't thank me yet. I'll come over here in the morning and do some figuring. We can talk for real tomorrow afternoon when I get home from work."

"Perfect." She grinned.

He pushed open the front door. "You coming?"

She was halfway through the bedroom door. "No, I think I'll stay and make some notes. I'll see you tomorrow."

He nodded. "See you then."

She heard the door close and stepped back into the main room to watch him go. He was so calm and so steady. She needed a friend like him. She just hoped he would still want to be her friend when he found out about the baby.

Her hand reflexively went to her abdomen. Whatever happened, she and her baby would be okay. She would make sure of it.

Chapter Four

The next afternoon, Latham was back in the cottage, taking some notes of his own. He let the tape measure slide into place with a snap and turned to his notepad on the countertop to write down the measurements. Wynn's idea of building a loft was actually pretty doable if he opened up the attic space.

A few industrial touches, a coat of white paint, and this shabby old place would look completely different.

The door behind him slowly swung open. Latham turned around to see a little boy around five or six years old, maybe, standing in the doorway, his thumb stuck in his mouth, a dirty bandage on his knee. Big brown eyes missed nothing as they perused the room.

"Hey, buddy, whatcha doin'? Anybody know where you are?"

The little dude still didn't say anything. Latham looked out the door toward the farmhouse to see if anyone was coming. No one was in sight. "So, you want to see what I'm doing?"

A nod. Communication established.

"I'm measuring because I'm going to build something that needs to fit in here. You want to help?"

Another solemn nod.

"Okay, I have one more measurement I need." Latham handed the end of the measuring tape to the little guy. "You take this over to that wall and we'll see how wide the room is."

The boy didn't respond, but he took the measuring tape to the wall and held it there. Latham made a quick measurement, which he would have to redo, but it did give him a basic idea. "Thanks, bud. You're a good helper."

Joe Sheehan appeared in the door. "Here you are, Matthew! I've been looking for you. Claire wants you to come back to the kitchen and finish your breakfast."

The little boy started for the door, but turned back to wave shyly at Latham.

Latham stuck his hand in his pocket and pulled out a small flexible measuring tape, no sharp edges. "Hey buddy, you take this one and see what you can find to measure inside."

A grin spread across the thin face, and Matthew grabbed the tape measure out of Latham's hand and sprinted for the house.

"Cute kid."

"He is cute. Also a total escape artist. Can't turn your back on him for a second." Joe walked to the refrigerator and pulled out a bottled water, tossing one to Latham and opening one for himself.

Latham took a long drink. "Thanks. You off work today?"

"I'm home today, but I'm learning I'm never completely off work. I've already fielded about four phone calls." Joe Sheehan was Wynn's older brother and moved back to town after an injury in the line of duty. Joe became the police chief of their little town, shortly after he'd fallen for Claire Conley.

The top cop looked around the small cabin. "I think I'd blocked out the neon green paint in the bathroom. It's really awful, isn't it? I hope Wynn's planning to repaint."

Latham grinned and leaned back on the kitchen island. "White everywhere. I wonder if she knows how many coats of paint it's going to take to cover that green."

"I could answer that, but I'm not going to.

A year of marriage under my belt has taught me that keeping my mouth shut is often the wisest policy." Joe laughed as he paced the length of the room, pausing to look out the window and take in the view of the farmhouse across the pond. He cleared his throat. "So, now that Wynn's back in town and you're helping her with the cottage, are you planning to ask her out?"

Latham didn't move, just kept his eyes trained on Joe's face and tried not to smile. "I haven't really thought that far ahead. Right now we have a business arrangement between friends. If things change, I could update you."

"Sure. She was dead set on leaving Red Hill Springs when she graduated high school. Now things are different. Maybe you should follow through on that crush you had on her in high school." He looked around. "Wow, I forgot how quiet it is down here."

While Latham was processing the new-found knowledge that Joe had known about his infatuation with Wynn in high school, the door slammed open and a girl around seven years old came bursting through the door. "Joe! Claire said to come quick. Penny's little brother got his head stuck in the banisters again!"

Joe sighed and shot a look at Latham. "So much for quiet."

As Joe swung the little one onto his shoulders, he was rewarded with a pure, sweet giggle, and the look on his face was anything but annoyed. Yeah, Red Hill Springs' police chief definitely had a soft side. Latham remembered when all the mamas in town warned their kids to stay away from Joe. He'd turned out pretty good despite all the dire warnings.

They'd all changed since they roamed this small town as kids. Maybe those changes were for the better, maybe some not so much. He wondered again what brought Wynn back to Red Hill Springs. And if she was really going to stay.

Latham shrugged into his coat and stuck the tape measure in his pocket. He followed Joe around the trail to where he'd parked his old truck in the driveway. As he drove home, his ideas for the cabin turned in his mind. He could almost imagine the space the way it would look after the reno. Wynn would be at her easel in the loft studio, maybe a pot of coffee on in the kitchen.

It was sentimental, sure, but he always tried to think about the people he was building for. A house wasn't a home until someone made it one. The tables he created in his barn workshop were only wood and nails until they became the centerpiece of a family kitchen.

Latham turned into the drive on his property, his mind on a big fire and a cup of coffee. He'd stayed longer than he'd meant to at the cottage, and the shadows were long over the gravel road. He hoped Wynn wasn't too bored. Maybe he was asking too much of her. Although, now that he'd seen how big the job she had in mind for him was, he wasn't as worried about that.

The dogs barreled around the corner of the house as they heard his door open. He gave them a quick scratch and hurried to the door, pushing it open to find Wynn at the kitchen table putting Scrabble tiles into their velvet bag.

She looked up with a smile. "Well, hey. Your pop was just starting to get worried about you."

"Was not." Pop's voice came from around the corner.

Latham shook his head. "He wasn't too much trouble?"

"No, he was not." The grumpy voice came from the living room again.

"Maybe he's hungry?" Wynn suggested.

Pop stuck his head back into the kitchen. "Yes, as a matter of fact, he is hungry."

Latham ignored his unruly grandpa. "So he was okay today?"

"He was great. He beat me at Scrabble. Apparently, I need to brush up on my vocabulary." Wynn walked into the kitchen, lifted the lid on the slow cooker and stirred something that smelled amazing before grabbing her purse and jacket from the counter. "I guess I'll see you guys tomorrow. Bye, Pop."

The grizzly gray head popped back into the doorway. "See you tomorrow, Wynn."

Latham, still in his coat, followed her out the door, Teddy bumping his legs.

Frank dropped a grimy ball at Wynn's feet, and with a smile, she bent to pick it up. "You've got my number, don't you, Frank?"

With a quick movement, she hurled the ball into the yard and Frank tore off after it. "He knows I can't resist his goofy grin."

"Please stay and eat some of the dinner you cooked. It's only fair."

She paused on the walkway. "I've got to head home tonight, but rain check?"

Across the yard, Frank scooped up the ball and ran full speed across the yard. Latham could see the trajectory of his path, and the seventy-pound dog was bearing down on Wynn, like a runaway train.

Just as Frank reached them, Latham dove

between him and Wynn, grabbing the dog and spinning so that he landed on his back and not on top of the dog. Frank scrambled away.

Wynn rushed to his side, tripped over his boot and landed on his chest with a rush of air.

His arms closed reflexively around her, and her eyes locked with his. "Wynn—"

Frank dropped the nasty, wet tennis ball by Latham's shoulder, and somehow understanding he had a captive audience, slurped a big kiss into Wynn's ear.

She squealed and rolled to the ground on her back, laughing when Teddy joined Frank in planting wet, slobbery kisses on her face.

Latham shooed the dogs, who were highly annoyed that their plan to lick Wynn into a puddle of laughter had been thwarted. He pulled Wynn to her feet. Her hair was scattered over her shoulders, her cheeks pink as she leaned over to scratch behind the ears of his two misbehaving dogs.

She was laughing.

He was poleaxed.

How was it that he hadn't seen her for years and as soon as he did, the feelings he thought he'd squelched years ago came roaring back?

He cleared his throat, forcing his brain to

make words as she found her car keys again. "Sorry about that. Pop's companion calls them hooligans, and they really are."

"I'll see you tomorrow around noon. Hope you and Pop have a good night."

He waited to make sure her car started and gave her a wave as he turned toward the house. Teddy bumped his leg and whined. "I know, Ted. Believe me, I know."

Wynn paused in the driveway at Red Hill Farm when she heard her name called. She'd spent the morning in her new home and had a sketchbook full of ideas to show for it. Was it nesting if it happened before she even had a baby bump?

Jordan, in jeans and riding boots, hugged the fence on an enormous brown horse.

"I was hoping you'd be here today!" Wynn walked to the fence. The big horse sniffed her hair and snorted.

Jordan laughed. "I've had Rocco here out for a run. He's here on a trial basis so we can see if he's a fit for our therapy program."

"How's it going?"

Jordan slid to the ground and scratched under the horse's mane, laughing when he leaned in to her touch. "He's amazing. Really calm and responsive. I'm a little concerned about his size, especially with the kids, but we could probably make it work."

As Jordan took the tack off Rocco, Wynn crossed her arms on the top bar of the fence. "I've been making notes about the cottage. I can't wait to have it ready to move into. I love being at Mom's, but if I'm going to figure out my life, I need to be in my own place."

"I heard from Ash that you're working for Latham, taking care of his pop." Jordan plopped the saddle onto a stand and rolled her shoulders.

"Yes. He asked if I could help, and we made a deal—his carpentry skills for my time with Pop. I definitely got the better end of the deal. Pop is awesome." Wynn grinned. "And I have a really long list of things for Latham to do out here."

"I also heard there was something between you and Latham, you know, once upon a time." Jordan stopped brushing long enough to give Wynn a long, speculative look.

Wynn was going to kill her brother. "You heard wrong. Mostly wrong," she amended. "Besides, it wouldn't matter. I'm not the person I was back then, and I'm not sure he would like the person I am now."

"Hey, you're working on it. None of us is perfect. It's like this horse. He's going to make a great therapy horse, but I wouldn't put a kid up on him right now for a million dollars. He's got the temperament, but developing the skills takes time."

"You're comparing me to a horse?"

With a shrug, Jordan laughed. "Hey, I work with what I've got. Plus I like most horses better than most people."

"So it was a compliment." Wynn laughed and grimaced as she looked at her watch. "I'd love to stay to see what kind of farm animals you'll be comparing me to next, but I promised Mom I'd be home for dinner tonight. She's testing out a new recipe for the café."

"Don't suppose she needs any more testers?"

"You know she always makes enough food for an army. Come on over."

"I'll text Ash and see if he and Levi want to meet me there." She snapped her fingers, and Rocco rolled his eyes back at her. "I almost forgot, do you think you could keep Levi for me tomorrow?"

"Absolutely, if I can take him to Latham's with me."

"Yeah, that's no problem. Just make sure the space is baby proof. He's into everything now."

"I love that. And, of course, I'll make sure

the place is totally Levi-proof." She started for the car. "Text me if you're coming to dinner and I'll set three more places."

"Look, I know you didn't ask my opinion." Inwardly, Wynn sighed as Jordan tied Rocco off and walked to the fence. "Being pregnant doesn't make you a bad person, but hating yourself can cripple you."

Tears flashed in Wynn's eyes. She swiped them away. "Yeah, thanks for activating the pregnancy hormones."

Jordan didn't smile, but her eyes were soft with sympathy. "I have some experience with a lack of self-confidence. Have you told Latham about the baby?"

"No." Wynn looked at the ground, resisted the urge to kick a tuft of grass. "I just…don't want to."

"Tell him. He's going to hear it from someone else if you don't."

"I know. And I will."

Jordan made a face. "Sorry for telling you what to do. It's a familial hazard, so I guess you'll get used to it."

"Not a bad deal since you come along with the advice."

Wynn walked to the car, her thoughts tumbling in her mind. She'd had a lot of acquaintances in DC, but no one she'd call a friend.

She was lucky that her brother picked someone she wanted to be friends with.

Jordan's words nagged at her, too. She saw Latham every day, and the longer she waited to tell him, the more awkward it was going to be. She had to tell him tomorrow, and just thinking about the conversation made her stomach churn. In a few short days, she'd come to depend on him. What if telling him meant the end of their renewed friendship?

Latham knew they were home because Wynn's car was in the driveway. There were embers glowing in the fireplace, so he knew they'd been in the family room where Pop was usually holed up, if he wasn't in the sunroom minding his "store."

He walked out the back door and found them on the porch. The sun had started to fade, but the two of them stood outside, Wynn apparently having forgotten the lesson she learned about playing fetch with his dogs.

She threw the ball, and the two big dogs took off. Latham heard an infectious giggle and realized that Ash and Jordan's little boy was there, too. He was bouncing in Pop's arms and laughing at the dogs as they tore across the yard.

Latham had to stop and collect himself for

a second. Not only was Pop not inside in his chair dozing through life, he was actually participating in it, holding little Levi with a smile on his face. Signs of life, the doctor would've said. Latham had nearly given up on ever seeing them again.

He slipped back into the house to make a pot of coffee.

A few minutes later, the door opened. Pop came in, still carrying the little boy, talking to Wynn over his shoulder. "If you get Levi some juice, I'll sit in the rocker with him."

"And for you?"

"I wouldn't mind a little sip of juice, myself."

"Hey, I didn't know you were here." Wynn joined Latham in the kitchen. She uncapped a sippy cup and rinsed it in the sink.

"I just came in, but I didn't want to interrupt. Pop seems really engaged."

"He was really present today. He and Levi hit it off, so I think that helped." She poured juice into the cup and capped it before pulling another plastic cup out of the cabinet and filling it with juice also.

A second after she'd taken the cups into the family room, she motioned for Latham to join her. He peeked around the corner and saw Pop sound asleep in the recliner with

Levi asleep on his chest, one small pudgy arm wrapped around Pop's neck.

"I'll just put these in the fridge for later." Wynn's smile lingered as she walked back into the kitchen.

"Join me for a cup of coffee? It's decaf this time of day."

"Sure."

As he poured the coffee, he laughed. "I was thinking the other day about the time you hid under Ash's bed and tickled his face with a feather every time he started to drift off. Joe and I were watching through a crack in the door and finally woke him up because we were laughing so hard. You were an evil genius."

"Me? What about the time you and Joe set off the smoke alarm with a cigarette and blasted Ash with a Super Soaker when he came running out of his room?"

He slid the mug in front of her. "One hundred percent Joe's idea."

"Whose idea was it to hide Jules's cat in the dishwasher?"

Latham choked on his coffee. "I had no part in that!"

"Me, either." She crossed her heart in the air and took a tentative sip of coffee. "We had some fun times, though."

"We really did."

"I had such an awful crush on you that I could barely stammer. It made me so mad because when have I ever not been able to speak my mind?"

He was quiet, spinning the mug in slow circles. "Why'd you come back, Wynn? Ever since high school, all you could talk about was leaving. Why come home now?"

The coffee burned in her throat, the question she'd been dreading hanging in the air. Latham's house was cozy, the fire burning low in the family room, the lights glowing warm against the gray winter afternoon sky. She longed to stay right here in this moment, before she answered the question he asked.

"It's okay, Wynn," he said, gently. "If you don't want to talk about it, it's fine."

She looked up from the black coffee and into his face. His eyes on hers were warm and safe, like his home, like him… They lingered on hers with a hint of curiosity but mostly understanding. The thing she hated the most was to see that look fade from his eyes.

Unblinking, she blurted. "I'm pregnant."

A horn honked outside. Levi woke up with a start, wailing in Pop's arms. Wynn hurried into the family room to pick up the little boy.

Jordan blew into the house like a whirlwind, Levi diving into her arms. They were gone almost as quickly as she came, Wynn swept along with them, stopping only long enough to grab her keys from the counter and send Latham an apologetic look.

Following Jordan's dust trail down the long driveway, Wynn took in a deep breath, her window down, letting in the bracing January-cold air.

A person who wasn't a coward would've stayed for the conversation. But Wynn had seen the shocked expression on Latham's face when she told him she was pregnant.

She didn't need to hear the disappointment in his voice.

Chapter Five

Wynn perched on a stool in the kitchen at Take the Cake, with a cup of herbal tea cooling on the table. Her sister, Jules, was using a tool to core the cupcakes for filling. "What kind are those?"

"Caramel apple. Apple filling, caramel frosting." Jules had her hair, a slightly darker version of Wynn's, tucked into a tidy bun. Everything about Jules was tidy. She picked up a piping bag and filled the cupcakes with quick efficient motions. When she had them all filled and frosted, she slid one over to Wynn.

"I was hoping you would let me taste test." Wynn took a bite. "Jules, this is incredible. Like seriously."

"I've been working on the combo for a while." Jules slid the tray of cupcakes into the cooler and pulled out another tray, this one full of red velvet cupcakes, which she began frosting with a different piping bag. "So what did Latham say when you told him you're expecting?"

"I left before he could say anything at all. I just didn't want to deal, and yes, I know—I'm a coward."

Jules's eyes softened. "It's okay. Anyone would feel the same way."

Wynn choked on her tea. "Um, how would you know? You never got in trouble, even when we were kids."

Jules threw a kitchen towel at Wynn, who snatched it with a laugh.

"Mom isn't super happy with me right now. With Claire getting so close to her due date, Mom is helping her with the other kids more and more. She asked me to keep an eye on the Hilltop and I am, but I can't keep up with both businesses forever, and I told her that yesterday."

Wynn frowned. "No wonder you have circles under your eyes."

"Thanks a lot." Jules didn't look up from the cupcakes, but continued piping a steady swirl of cream cheese frosting on each one.

"I'm kidding. Kind of. What's your plan?"

"Since I don't have one, let's talk about

you some more. It makes me feel better." The bell on the front door jingled, and Jules grimaced. "My front counter person isn't coming in until ten."

"I'll get this one. Finish those up so I can buy a few to take home." Wynn pushed open the door from the kitchen to the front room, a smile on her face for the customer. Latham stood in the small room, larger than life, his hands shoved in the pockets of his jeans.

Her stomach flipped.

And then he turned, and she knew the second he saw her.

"Wynn." His voice was thick with emotion.

She fought back a feeling of panic. She needed things to be okay with him. She didn't know why it was so important. It shouldn't be. She shouldn't want to run to him. Deliberately she kept the bakery counter between them.

"Latham, I'm sorry. I should've told you. I just didn't want to—"

He took three steps forward and stopped her words with a hand over hers. "Can we go for a walk?"

She nodded and called through the door to the kitchen. "Jules, I'm leaving. It's all clear out here."

"Thanks—I'll bring you any leftover cupcakes." Jules appeared in the door, sending Wynn a wide-eyed look when she caught sight of Latham standing in the entrance.

Latham held the front door open for Wynn, and she walked through it. Her mind was racing, in circles, because she didn't know what he was going to say, if he would be accusing or accepting.

Angry or kind.

The sun was shining, but the cold was biting. She shivered, and he took his scarf off and wrapped it around her neck, leaving her enveloped in the scent of pine and coffee and, well, man.

They walked slowly down the sidewalk, under the awnings of the Main Street stores. He was quiet, and she searched her mind for something—anything—to say. "Don't you have to work today?"

"Not this morning. One of Pop's buddies came by for coffee and dominoes, so I took the opportunity to come and find you."

She glanced over at him. His cheeks were ruddy in the cold wind. "Because you want an explanation?"

"No, Wynn. I want to be your friend." His voice held the tiniest edge of exasperation. He turned into the courtyard in the church, and she saw a wooden bench tucked into an alcove, out of the wind. "I repaired this for the church a couple of years ago. It's a nice spot."

She sat down on one edge of the bench as far as she could possibly get from him. He stretched out his long denim-clad legs and sat in stillness. The laughter and squeals of the children at the elementary school carried to her on the wind and birds chattered in the courtyard, but Latham didn't speak.

She stared into the distance until she couldn't stand his patient silence any longer. "All of my life I wanted to work to make other people's lives better. I wanted to break molds and shatter glass ceilings." She blew out a breath. "Instead I've become the worst kind of cliché."

He leaned back and stretched his arm along the back of the seat. "I don't even know what that means."

"I had an affair with my boss. I thought he loved me. I promise you, I couldn't have been more wrong." Her voice still shook when she talked about it, and she despised the weakness it showed.

In contrast, Latham's voice was even and calm. "Does he know about the baby?"

"Yes."

His next words were slow and measured. "Does he want to be involved?"

When she'd told Preston that she was pregnant, he'd gone ice cold, stalking to his desk to write her a check to "take care of it."

She shook her head. "No. I think it's safe to say that he wants nothing to do with the baby. Or me."

"So you're home and you're staying." His expression was carefully neutral, and she ached that he felt the need to be so cautious, but she understood it. She hadn't seen anyone in Red Hill Springs in years, except her family when she'd flown in for a couple of days at Christmas or sometimes Thanksgiving.

She looked at him, allowing him to see the regret. "Honestly, I don't have any idea what my long-term plan is. This situation—" she waved a hand in the general area of her stomach "—is just so complicated."

Latham kind of half laughed and pressed his fingers into his temples. "Well, at least I know what to expect this time."

"I guess I deserved that." The number one person she hadn't wanted to see when she came home for visits—because of how she'd treated him when she left—was sitting right next to her. She'd dreamed for years of getting out of Red Hill Springs, Alabama. No one could've changed her mind about leaving—except for maybe Latham. And she hadn't been willing to take that chance. Instead she'd packed her bags, kissed her mom and dad and left on graduation night without saying goodbye.

Their fledgling romance hadn't had a chance because she hadn't given it one. She had no idea how to apologize after so many years.

He glanced at his watch. "I've got to go. I have an appointment in twenty minutes."

"I'll go out to your place to be with Pop." She pulled the scarf from her neck and held it out to him.

He shook his head, his eyes dark on hers, a wry smile on his lips. "Keep it. It looks better on you, anyway."

When he walked out of the courtyard, she couldn't help but feel he was walking away from her. There was too much in the past to be overcome, too much difference in what they wanted out of life.

Saturday morning, Latham moved his checker and drained the last bit of coffee from his mug. It was his and Pop's habit to play a game of checkers when they got home from breakfast at the Hilltop. Today he'd made Pop breakfast at home. He just hadn't wanted to risk running into Wynn. It seemed like there was so much they weren't saying, so much subtext.

Pop shot him a sly look from under bushy eyebrows and picked up his piece. He jumped Latham twice and ended up on the last row on Latham's side with a handful of Latham's checkers. His grandpa smiled contentedly, leaned back in his chair and said, "King me."

Groaning, Latham took one of his checkers and stacked it on his grandpa's. "How do you do that? You can't remember what you had for breakfast yesterday and you kill me in checkers every single day."

"Maybe you just stink at checkers."

Latham choked on his coffee. "Could be."

"Or maybe your mind is on Wynn. I may be old and half-crazy, but I remember how you moped around when Wynn Sheehan left town."

Latham scowled and looked away from Pop's shrewd speculation. "Just play checkers, Pop, and leave the analyzing to the professionals."

"I don't see any professionals around here." Pop quickly won the game and lifted his coffee mug with a satisfied smile. "So, when's her baby due?"

Sucking in a breath, Latham considered that he should probably stop being surprised by Pop's instincts about people. Maybe it was his shopkeeper background. He'd had to know his customers, and he had, for more than forty years. "So when did you figure it out?"

"I don't remember." For a second, Pop looked confused. "What were we talking about?"

"Wynn."

"Right." Pop stared into his coffee, and when he looked up, his eyes were steady on Latham's. "So there's no father?"

Latham raised an eyebrow. "Well, there *is* a father."

"You know what I mean. No father stepping up to take responsibility."

"No."

Pop picked a piece of bacon off the table and took a bite. "A real man would. It's good she has you."

"Pop, I don't think she wants me or anyone." A fact that Latham had come to terms with years ago, or at least he thought he had.

"Why isn't this bacon crisp? Margenia never makes my bacon floppy." Pop's eyes clouded as he disappeared into the haze of confusion that had characterized the last few years. Latham sighed and slid the plate of leftover bacon off the table so it wouldn't upset Pop further.

Sometimes he imagined that things were getting better. Doctors had told them there had been no changes to Pop's brain. There was no medical explanation. After more than two years, Latham was used to these slip-backs into the past, but the truth was, he missed the relationship he'd had with his grandpa.

His grandpa who thought Latham should step forward and be a man for Wynn. He would. He wanted to be there for her as much as she would allow. Maybe the only thing he could do was be the friend that he knew she needed—if she would let him. She was so darn skittish around him, he didn't know if she'd let him get close.

A knock on the door surprised him. He looked at his watch. He wasn't expecting anyone.

He certainly wasn't expecting it to be Wynn on the other side of the door on a Saturday. She looked chic, even in jeans and a shirt with a vest, pulling a treat out of her large leather bag for the dogs who were bumping her relentlessly.

"Ah, now I see why you're their favorite visitor. I wasn't expecting to see you today."

She squared her shoulders. "You didn't get to spend the morning in your workshop yesterday because you were looking for me. So, I came to stay with Pop this morning so you can make up the time."

"You don't have to do that."

Wynn hitched her bag farther onto her shoulder. "I don't mind. I have a doctor's appointment in Mobile on Monday, so I won't be able to be here then."

He pushed the door open to let her in. "Well, in that case, please come in. Is anyone going with you to the appointment?"

"No." She followed him into the kitchen and set her bag down, paints and brushes spilling out onto the counter. She shrugged slightly. "I thought Pop might enjoy a diversion. It's not as cold today, but we can paint at the kitchen table if we need to."

"He had a good morning. We played checkers and he was with me, and then like a switch was flipped, he was gone." He'd never felt as powerless in his life as he did dealing with Pop's illness. All he could do, absolutely the only thing he could do, was be present for the conversations and the moments when they came.

Wynn's hand on his arm interrupted the self-recrimination. "He has a good life, Latham. He has you."

"Thank you." He cleared his throat. "If you're sure this is what you want to do, I do have some things I need to catch up on in my workshop."

"We'll be fine."

Latham watched as she walked into the living room where Pop stared at the game shows on TV. She touched his shoulder. "Hey, Pop, I'm going to hang out with you for a while. Do you need anything? Latham has a pot of coffee on in the kitchen."

He slipped out of the back door, his dogs at his heels. For the first time, maybe ever, he wanted to stay inside instead of being in his workshop buried to his elbows in sawdust.

Wynn was such an enigma to him. Maybe that's why he'd always been so fascinated with her. He'd been convinced after the conversation yesterday that he'd blown it with her again. And here she was this morning, looking so perfect and—what was the word?— *cosmopolitan*, that was it.

She was going to the doctor alone. Maybe that's the way she wanted it, but could be Pop was right. Maybe she did need someone just to stand beside her.

She had family here. A handful of sisters and sisters-in-law. She had no reason to need him.

But maybe she did.

He lifted a huge wide plank that used to be the floor in a two-hundred-year-old church and began to sand. Soon it would be a table for a family in Atmore.

As always, working with his hands soothed his ragged edges. He couldn't do anything about Pop except just be there for the moments that counted.

Wynn ran through her mental checklist as she was walking out the door. She had her insurance card and driver's license, a book loaded on her phone to read if she had to wait, and a bottle of water in her bag. She locked the door, turned around and stopped cold.

Latham stood on the front walk. He was wearing his typical jeans and work boots, flannel shirt and down vest for warmth, and he just looked so good. She walked closer. "What are you doing here?"

"Just hear me out. I know we're not a thing, and that's fine with me. But I also know you won't ask anyone to go with you today, even though you have like seventeen sisters."

She tried—and failed—to keep a straight face. "That's exaggerating a little."

He pulled the ball cap off his head and stabbed his fingers through his hair. "I'm going. If you won't let me into the building, I'll wait in the car, but I'm not letting you go by yourself."

"Okay." She surprised even herself, but she wasn't as surprised as he was.

"What? Okay? Okay. The truck's running. Heater's on."

She followed him down the drive, and when he opened the door for her, she slid into the seat. And realized he not only had the heater on, but the seat warmers, too. He'd gone to all this trouble, even to the point of taking a day off of work so that she wouldn't be alone.

Tears gathered in her eyes. She sniffed.

Latham jumped into his seat, took one look at her and freaked. "What's wrong? Did I say something? Are you upset?"

She laughed through the tears and sniffed again. "No, I'm fine. It was just a really nice thing for you to do, and I'm so hormonal. I cry at the drop of a hat."

Hormones were awful, that part was true, but the real answer to his question was she wasn't used to having someone to depend on. Even when she and Preston were at the height of their relationship, he wasn't dependable. *She* was.

It was her fault for letting him get away with it. Now she didn't care, she just didn't realize how much she missed having someone—anyone—who just cared about her. She'd been on her own a long time.

She sent a sidelong glance at Latham as he put the truck into gear and backed out of her drive. So it seemed she wasn't on her own anymore.

Chapter Six

Latham pulled into the parking lot at the Women's Medical Center. He'd give his favorite band saw to be anywhere but here. He hadn't had a lot of girlfriends, hadn't had that many dates, to be honest. Women were a mystery, and being here, in the middle of women's land…well, it was awkward, no way around it.

There'd been very little talking on the thirty-minute drive. He found a parking place and parked, leaving his hands on the wheel. Neither he nor Wynn made any movement toward the door handle.

He cleared his throat. "So, are you excited?"

Her hands twisted in her lap. "Nervous and excited, I guess. I want everything to be okay."

She still hadn't moved to open the door. Her eyes skittered to his and away again.

Latham took the keys out of the ignition. "You ready?"

"This just makes it seem so real." She whispered the words as she stared at the building.

Well, yeah. Okay, so he could admit it had to be weird…and weighty, growing a new life. He smiled at her and searched for the right words to reassure her. "You're going to rock this. I've never seen an obstacle you couldn't stare down, Wynn Sheehan. So let's go."

"I'm not one of your students. I don't need a pep talk." Wynn hadn't taken her eyes off the door to the building.

He laughed at her words. "Oh, really? Then why don't you stop acting like you need one?"

The barest hint of a smile curved one corner of her mouth. "I can do this."

"You can do this."

She drained her water bottle and got out of the car. He followed behind her as she walked through the door, signed in, filled out a million papers and, as she handed the clipboard over to the receptionist, her name was called.

"I'll be right here." He gestured around the waiting room, which was decorated like someone's grandmother's living room and filled with women who barely looked up from their phones.

He saw a brief wobble in her smile, but she nodded. "Okay."

He walked to an empty chair and grabbed the magazine that looked the least likely to be embarrassing and tried not to worry. She was going to be fine.

But when he looked up, she'd stopped in the door, and for a second he thought she was going to chicken out. She said something to the nurse and then walked back to him. "You can come, if you want."

If you want. Latham wasn't at all sure he wanted to. What was beyond that door seemed foreign and mystical. But he nodded and followed her into the patient area, where a woman in scrubs waited.

"I'm Cass. I'll be doing your ultrasound today, and if Dr. Reganza has time, she'll pop her head in for a look, as well." Cass showed them into a dim room with an examination table and a computer-looking machine and little else. He swallowed hard as he thought about Wynn lying on that table.

"So, Wynn, you'll change into the gown here on the exam table and I'll be right back." Cass opened another door on the other side of the room and disappeared.

Latham stood staring at his shoes for a

minute until he realized that Wynn was waiting on him so she could change.

"I'm sorry. Wow. I'll, uh, just be out here." He stepped into the hall, his face on fire. He'd definitely underestimated how awkward this was going to be.

He gave her a few minutes to change and then stepped inside the door as the technician came back in on the other side. She pointed at a chair on the other side of the exam table from where she would be sitting. "Dad, you can sit there."

"He's not the father," Wynn said, too quickly.

Cass's eyes didn't move from the monitor as she typed. "Okay, got it."

"He's…"

Latham wasn't sure what she was about to say…an old almost-boyfriend…my house renovator…on my brother's pick-up soccer team.

"…a friend and was kind enough to come with me today because I was nervous."

Cass smiled and glanced at him. "That's so nice."

Latham realized at that point that Cass had probably seen all kinds of relationships walk through that door and, in the scheme of things, his relationship with Wynn wasn't that weird. He settled back in the chair.

Cass pressed a small almost microphone-looking thing onto Wynn's slightly rounded abdomen. "There are some measurements that I'll be taking, so I'll be moving the transducer around. It might be a little hard to see what we're looking at, but I promise I've had lots of practice."

She slid the wand thing around to the bottom of Wynn's abdomen, and suddenly a whoosh-whoosh-whoosh filled the room. "Ah, there's our strong heartbeat. Sounds perfect. One-forty."

Latham's own heart was in his throat. That sound wasn't anything he'd expected to hear at this stage of pregnancy, but it was amazing. He couldn't think anything but *Thank You, Jesus, thank You.*

Cass slid the transducer farther around and clicked a few buttons. "You're measuring about sixteen weeks and three days." She pointed to the screen. "That line is your baby's femur."

Wynn didn't look at him, but her hand slid across the sheet and found his. He looked at their joined hands and thought *I have made a terrible misjudgment.*

He'd thought he could handle a simple trip to the doctor. He was a big boy, he'd gotten over his feelings for her a long time ago. But this—there was no preparing for this.

Cass made several more measurements and then said, "She's cooperating this morning. This is her arm and hand and—" she moved the transducer in a slight circle "—there's her little face."

"She?" Tears instantly formed in Wynn's eyes. "A little girl?"

Cass laughed. "Yep. Oh, look, she's got her finger in her mouth."

Wynn gasped and gripped his hand tighter, her eyes wide and shining, glued to the monitor. "Oh my goodness, she's just so perfect. Look at her, Latham. She's wiggling her fingers."

The 3-D image seemed to materialize slightly slower than real time as the baby moved, and it was grainy, but there was her sweet little face. So clear.

His eyes hazed with tears. He could barely see. "She's beautiful."

"She is." Wynn looked up. Her eyes were dark in the dim room, but they were shimmering with emotion. "She's amazing. And I'm her mother."

She stared at the screen as if trying to memorize the tiny features.

"I'm her mother," she repeated.

Cass moved the transducer across Wynn's belly one final time. "We're done for today. Dr. Reganza must've gotten busy, but she'll review this and let you know if she has any concerns. Otherwise, I'll let them know at the front desk to set up an appointment for you in one month."

Latham rubbed his thumb and fingers across his lashes, erasing any remaining sign of dampness, and cleared his throat. "I'll just meet you back in the waiting room."

He slipped out the door and into the waiting area, where he dropped into a chair, his mind reeling. At no time had he considered that seeing Wynn's baby would rock his world the way it had.

His heart had been in his throat, and he couldn't take his eyes off the tiny features. Wynn's hand gripping his was the realest thing he'd ever felt.

Shell-shocked, he stared blankly at the window until he heard the door open from the patient area in the back. Wynn stopped at the reception desk, and the Wynn he knew was back, confident and in control.

Would that moment of vulnerability and the connection they'd made last? He wasn't sure he wanted to know the answer to that. Maybe he should take a step back, although he didn't know how to do that since she was literally in his house every day.

She turned away from the desk and smiled at him. He'd already had to survive losing her once. Was he really prepared to do that again?

Wynn sat in the sun on her sister-in-law Claire's back porch and watched the kids play. She was supposed to be sketching, but honestly, she was mostly just letting her thoughts drift, her hand resting on her belly. Now that she knew she was having a healthy baby, she felt released to let herself dream a little.

She almost hadn't dared believe that she was pregnant. Hadn't wanted to believe it sometimes. She'd blown her life up with her actions. It would be easy to blame someone else, but she had to take responsibility for what she had done.

How gracious was God that she would be given the opportunity to be the mama of the baby girl growing inside her?

The sound of laughter drifted to her from where Pop was sitting at the picnic table helping Aleecya with her homework. Wynn laughed, too, as she saw Aleecya give Pop a high five.

Someone tapped at her shoulder. Seven-year-old Penny was trying to quit sucking her thumb and had a Band-Aid wrapped around it. She whispered to Wynn, "I want the grandpa to do my math with me."

The grandpa. Wynn wondered if Penny had ever had a grandpa. If she had, she was certainly missing him now. "Why don't you ask him if he's feeling up to it?"

Big blue eyes opened wide, and she shook her head with a vehemence that sent her two ponytails bouncing. "Can you ask him? It's double numbers and it's really hard."

"Sure. Come on." Wynn stood and Penny slid her hand into Wynn's larger one. Penny's hand was small and soft and so trusting. Wynn swallowed hard. Before too long, her own daughter's hand would be sliding into hers.

What would her daughter be like? Would she have white-blond hair like Wynn had as a child? Would she have the famous Sheehan blue eyes?

At the picnic table, Wynn sat beside Pop, her feet facing away from the table, his underneath it. She studied his face. He didn't look tired. His blue eyes, sometimes so distant and hazy, didn't look confused. They sparkled. "Hey, Pop, when you and Aleecya are finished, Penny here would like 'the grandpa' to give her some help with her math homework."

He turned to Penny. "You would?"

She nodded, her thumb creeping to her mouth and back again when she remembered the Band-Aid.

His eyes met Wynn's, and she could see the compassion there for a little girl who just needed a grandpa. He pretended to think about it. "My friends call me Pop. I'm pretty good at math. You have to be when you own a store."

Her eyes widened. "You own a store? Does it have candy?"

He laughed. "It used to, when it was open."

A frown creased his forehead, and Wynn had a moment of panic that he was going to slide away from them. "Pop, Penny is adding double numbers. It's really hard."

Aleecya slammed her book, and Pop looked up. "I'm done with mine. Thanks, Pop!"

She stopped in her stride toward the house to give Pop a quick squeeze around the neck. His eyes widened and then got suspiciously shiny. "You're welcome, little missy. You're very smart and you'll catch on in no time."

Aleecya beamed. "Will you be back tomorrow?"

Pop glanced at Wynn, who nodded and shrugged. "I can be."

"Okay, see ya then!" The teen, who'd had

precious little positive male influence in her life, skipped toward the house.

Pop bent his head over Penny's math page. "Well, then. Let's see about those double numbers."

Wynn smiled and started back to her chair on the porch. She stopped short when she saw Latham standing there, his tool belt over his shoulder and an expression on his face like he'd been struck by lightning.

She walked closer, placing a hand on his arm. "What's wrong?"

"I haven't seen him that happy in years. He's been moving from one recliner to the other with his crossword." His voice was a little shaky.

"It's good to be outdoors. I'll get him home shortly. As fun as the children are, they're also exhausting."

"When he's like this, it almost makes me think he could be getting better. I know that's probably impossible, but I want it so badly." A fleeting smile crossed his face as he watched his Pop being so patient with sweet Penny.

He took a breath and squared his shoulders. "I'm headed to the cottage for an hour or two. Will you still be here?"

"No. I'll take Pop home and get him some supper. You take your time. I mean, you know." She laughed. He was working on her soon-to-be home and she was telling him to take his time.

He grinned and started toward the house. From behind her, a little boy yelled and ran toward Latham, who dropped his tool belt and took a few minutes to toss the football, even though he had work to do.

Wynn breathed a small sigh. Such kindness that was just ingrained in him. It came from his heart with barely a thought. It just was.

Claire opened the back door and stepped out onto the porch, a glass of sweet tea in her hand. "Mind if I sit with you for a minute?"

Wynn's eyes opened wide. She jumped to her feet. "Do you mind keeping an eye on Pop and Penny for a sec? I've got to…there's just something I've got to do."

"Yeah, okay, sure." The bewildered look on Claire's face didn't slow Wynn down.

She needed to talk to Latham right now.

Latham tossed his tool belt onto the island in the cottage, placed his palms flat on the cool granite surface and let his head drop. He was almost ready to call in his work crew to do the build-out, so he wanted to make sure there were no questions about the build that he didn't know the answer to. But first he needed a minute—just a minute—to process. Pop seemed to come to life before his eyes. Wynn and the baby. Her baby.

The door slammed against the wall and Wynn stood in the opening, her hair a little wild, eyes a little wild, too.

He jerked upright. "What's wrong? Is it Pop?"

"No. I just—I had to talk to you. I've let this go for so long. I thought it would make things less hard or less complicated or something. But instead I feel like there's this huge wall between us, a wall that I built because of what I did ten years ago."

His shoulders relaxed. Now she wanted to talk about this? "It's fine. It's over."

She took two steps closer. "It's not fine. I hurt you, and I'm so deeply sorry."

"Wynn. I forgive you. I forgave you a long time ago. Is that what you want to hear?" He was so tired that he forgot—didn't have the bandwidth, really—to filter his thoughts.

"You deserve to know what really happened that night."

"I was there, Wynn. I think I know what happened."

On the night she graduated, while some kids had a bonfire by the river, they sat on a floating dock, their feet in the water, talking, dreaming. Moon shining on the water, music playing in the distance, magic.

When he kissed her it felt like the most perfect, most right thing in the world. All his life he'd told himself she was off-limits, but in that moment, he'd been willing to take on her brothers. Truth, he'd have taken on the whole football team if he had to if it meant he could be with her.

He looked in her eyes, and he could see the wonder and the emotion. She felt the same way.

One of her friends had called to her from the bonfire, and she'd obligingly gotten to her feet, laughing at some crazy antic. She'd looked back at him with regret, and he'd smiled at her. No worries, he'd said, we can talk tomorrow. We have all the time in the world.

The next day, he'd dropped by her house, palms sweaty, to see her, to face her brothers. Instead he found out she'd left. Not a word. No goodbye, no explanation. Just gone.

He looked away, staring beyond her at the spring-fed pond. The surface was just turning pink as the sun began to set, ripples spreading as a frog jumped into the water. She put her hand on his arm, and he took a deep breath. "What can you possibly say now that will make a difference? We're fine. I got over this a long time ago."

"I was so in love with you. I had been for years, all of high school at least. When you kissed me that night, I could see it all unfolding—dating each other through college, then a wedding, a house, a couple of kids. And I didn't just see it—I *wanted* it."

"It was just a *kiss*, Wynn." Frustration had his shoulders edging up again.

"It wasn't. Not to me. That kiss scared the daylights out of me because for longer than I'd been wanting you, I'd dreamed of getting out of Red Hill Springs and making a difference in the world. I had no idea what that even meant, I just knew I had to do it."

He shrugged, honestly not seeing the connection. "Okay."

"If you'd asked me to stay, I would have. I would have thrown away a scholarship to Columbia for a full ride to the University of South Alabama. I would've spent my summers with you at the creek and Christmas holidays snuggled by the fire at my parents' house. And I would've loved it." Emotion twisted her face as she battled to keep it under control. "But I would've known that somewhere out there, an opportunity had been there waiting and I'd missed it."

Tears brimmed in her eyes, and he wondered how they could just hang there. He looked away. He didn't want to hear this.

"So I left. I packed a bag and went to stay with my great-aunt in Upstate New York for the summer and started at Columbia in the fall. And I tried to put you and what we could've had out of my mind. I tried to forget you."

He'd never felt more forgettable in his life. Here he was dressed in his work boots and jeans, a flannel over his favorite ragged-out T-shirt. He spread his work-rough hands wide. "I think you accomplished that. I didn't hear from you or see you until I walked into the Hilltop a few weeks ago."

Wynn shook her head. "No, I didn't accomplish it. That's what I'm trying to tell you. I didn't see you when I was home because I knew what I did to you was wrong."

He took a deep breath. "Okay, so you've apologized. It was just a kiss, Wynn. I wasn't planning white-picket fences and two-point-five kids."

She backed away from him and nodded. "That's fair. Maybe it was all in my head.

Maybe I made it seem like so much more than it was because my feelings for you were so big. Either way, I'm sorry for what I did."

He looked at his watch and glanced out the door. Dusk had fallen, and it was getting late. "I've got to go. I'll take Pop with me."

Her blue eyes were huge, and she looked fragile in a way he'd never seen her before. "Of course. I'm sorry I kept you so long."

"I'll see you tomorrow." He slung his tool belt over his shoulder, walked out the door and onto the porch, every step feeling like the wrong direction. The lights were on in the huge old farmhouse, and he knew that was where Pop waited, and he took a couple more steps. He should go in and get his grandpa and go home, to his life.

He stopped, dropped his tool belt on the path by the pond and strode back into the house. Wynn was at the fireplace.

Without any real conscious thought, he crossed the room, slid his fingers in her hair and took her mouth. He poured every unrequited feeling he'd ever had into that kiss, and when she sagged against him, he slid his arm around the small of her back and dragged her closer.

When he finally let her feet slide to the floor, he pressed a kiss into her hair and slid his thumb down the side of her flawless cheek. He took a step back, his hands, gentle now, sliding down her arms. "It wasn't just a kiss."

Chapter Seven

Wynn wound her way through the tables at the Hilltop, an easy smile on her face and a pot of coffee in her hand. Pop's sister had come to stay with him for a week or two, so she wouldn't be going to Latham's today, which was just as well. She had no idea what she would say to him since she was still reeling from that kiss last night.

In the past few weeks, she thought she'd finally managed to put Latham firmly in the friend category. That illusion—or delusion—had been shattered in a matter of seconds last night.

Catching herself staring out the front window, she startled. *Get it together, Wynn.* This wasn't ten years ago, and it was not last night. She was in the present, and that didn't include daydreaming about what might have been.

Tightening her grip on the coffeepot, she stopped by Mayor Campbell's table. "Freshen you up, Mayor?"

The older man, who'd lost his wife while Wynn had been away, held his cup out. "We need to have coffee together some time, Wynn. I know I'm just in local politics, but I'd enjoy picking your brain about what's going on in Washington these days."

"I'd love that, Mayor Campbell." She filled his mug with black coffee and dropped a few creamers from her apron pocket onto the table.

"Call me Chip, please. I'm hopeless at a schedule, so if you'll call my assistant, she'll put you on the calendar and I'll look forward to it."

Mayor Campbell—Chip—understated his involvement in politics. He might be a local mayor but he was a big player in his political party in this state, and Wynn relished the idea of chatting with him. He'd always had a soft spot for her, but would he feel the same about her when the word was out about her pregnancy? People may not know for sure who the father was, but there would certainly be speculation about her relationship with her former boss.

The bell on the door jingled. When she

looked up, Latham stood in the doorway. He was dressed in his usual jeans, boots and flannel. There was nothing slick or fancy about him, but he oozed effortless masculinity. Her skin prickled, and she imagined it was the nerve endings relaying the message to her brain. *Stay away—this one is dangerous.*

When he caught sight of her, his eyes warmed. She turned away. She had no business being attracted to him—to his mind or heart or anything else.

She slid the coffeepot onto the warmer, and after a deep breath she turned back to him, a breakfast menu in hand. "We're not super busy. You're welcome to find a table."

He leaned on the counter, so close to her she could count his breaths. "I'm not here for a table."

The implication was that he was here for something else. Her heart raced despite the absolute futility of what he was hinting at and the talk she'd just had with herself.

He leaned so close that she could see the green and gold flecks in his deep brown eyes. "Come out with me tonight. I have a class to teach at six, and then we could get dinner somewhere and really talk. We can do something right this time."

It was tempting, so tempting. She'd love to go on a normal date, to pretend for a little while that nothing in her life had changed. But it had, and pretending otherwise wouldn't help anyone. Especially Latham. She shook her head slowly. "Latham, I can't go on a date with you."

"Why not?" Vulnerability flickered in his eyes before he shuttered it, and she resisted the urge to reach out to him.

She could feel a dozen pairs of eyes on them. "Come with me."

Grabbing him by the hand, she pulled him into her mother's office, a ruthlessly organized utilitarian space. "Look, you made your point last night. It *was* more than a kiss. There was something between us back then, something that could've probably been amazing. But that's the past, Latham. This baby I'm carrying is my present. I don't have the luxury of anything else."

Determination flared to life in his eyes. She knew it because she'd seen it before. "Latham, stop."

Instead of backing away, he took a step closer. "I'm not an immature schoolboy anymore, Wynn. I let you go once without a fight, and I'm not doing that again. We let this run its course and we decide it's not for us, fine, but we let it run its course."

Was he actually so thickheaded that he didn't understand why this was such a bad idea? "Latham, you can't date me! Your life is here. You teach at the college. I'm not married and I'm pregnant with another man's baby."

The words were hard and hung in the air. He had to see the truth. He was such a good person, truly a good person, the kind of person who gave up the life he'd planned so he could take care of his aging grandpa.

She was scarred and broken and trying to rebuild who she was. Trying to find some semblance of the self she respected.

Latham smiled, a lazy upturn of his lips, and the danger alert went off in her brain again. He took a step closer. "You can't scare me away, Wynn. I'll see ya around."

He left, and the air left with him. She sank into her mother's desk chair. She'd seen what happened when Latham turned the full force of his personality onto a goal. She'd just never been at the center of his sights before.

Latham slammed the board into position and hammered it down. He'd gone to Wynn with his heart on his sleeve and once again she'd tossed it back in his face, just a little more personally this time.

He went for the next board, ran it through the table saw with a satisfying buzz and squeal. He dropped it on the crossbeams and hammered the nails in, the sound reverberating around him.

Sweating now, he stripped off the flannel shirt and tossed it aside. He wasn't angry, exactly. He was frustrated. Frustrated that even after the last few weeks with him, she didn't trust him enough to take a chance and just go to dinner with him. Steak and a baked potato. He wasn't asking her to marry him.

The thought stuck in his mind like a tantalizing dream. A dream farther out of reach than the ones he normally tortured himself with. Dreams like finishing his PhD and making his living as a professor of history and political science.

He ran the next board through the saw with grim precision and then muscled it into place. He hammered the nails, feeling the blows all the way up to his shoulder.

When the ringing of the hammer stopped, he heard a voice behind him. "What are you doing?"

Turning toward it, he found Ash leaning casually against the porch rail, a baby monitor in his hand. "What does it look like I'm doing?"

"It looks like you're destroying a few boards."

Latham narrowed his eyes. "I'm building Levi a sandbox."

"With a deck?" Ash pushed off the railing and took the couple of steps down to the yard. At Latham's look, he raised both his hands. "Hey, I'm not complaining. Just asking."

"I needed to do something, and there are people at my house." Ash was staring at him like he'd never seen him before. "What?"

"I've just never seen you so—worked up. You're usually the calm one."

"I am calm." Latham resented the implication here. He dropped his safety goggles into place and shoved a board through the table saw.

Sawdust sprayed, and Ash brushed an invisible speck off his crisp dress shirt. "Of course you are. I heard you saw Wynn at the Hilltop this morning."

"Do we gossip like little girls now?"

Ash crossed his arms, an irritated look crossing his too-handsome face. "I'm not the one who nearly kissed someone in the middle of the local café in front of half the town."

Latham shoved the safety glasses back. "Your sister—"

"—is having a really hard time right now."

The words stopped Latham midsentence, pulling the plug on his frustration and draining it away. He closed his mouth.

Ash flipped the switch on the table saw, and the humming stopped. "Come on. Let's get a drink."

Latham followed Ash onto the porch and sank into one of the rockers that Jordan had placed there after she and Ash were married. Ash went into the house and returned with a couple of diet sodas. Latham cracked one open and took a long drink while Ash did the same.

They sat in silence for a while, the need for conversation never that pressing between the two of them who had been friends for so long.

Finally, Ash said, "Do you want to talk about it?"

"No." Latham scowled. He didn't want to talk about it. "Why aren't you at work?"

"The office closes at twelve on Wednesdays." Ash smiled without looking at Latham, but he lifted the baby monitor and waggled it. "I'm on duty here this afternoon. Levi's napping."

"I'm leaving. I didn't mean to disturb you." Latham drained the soda and stood. "I'll be back to finish Levi's sandbox."

He packed up his saw and put it into the back of his truck, slamming the tailgate before rounding the side and opening the driver's-side door.

"Latham." Ash stepped off the porch and walked closer. "If chasing Wynn is some kind of challenge to yourself to see if you can actually get her to care about you this time around, stop."

Latham leaned on his truck. "You really think that about me?"

"Truthfully, no. But Wynn was always the one who got away from you."

He crossed his arms. "I don't see her as a challenge. Her coming home threw me, is all. I'm just trying to make sense of it."

Ash nodded slowly. "Look, we never talked about Wynn back then, and I would've probably called you a baby if we did because I was mature like that. Meeting Jordan... I've never wanted anything as bad as I wanted Jordan in my life forever. So, if you care about my sister and she's under your skin like Jordan's under mine, don't give up."

Latham grinned. "Are we talking about feelings?"

Ash looked around. "Yeah, we need to go hit some balls or something."

"I have an extra tool belt you can strap on."

"Very funny." A squawk came from the baby monitor, and Ash started for the house. "That's my cue. See ya."

Latham vaulted into his truck seat and slammed the door. He sat and stared at the river for a minute. Ash had just taken a dramatic turn from the usual message from Wynn's brothers.

Giving up on Wynn wasn't an option. Latham was fully aware that she came with strings attached. He didn't care about that. Maybe there was something there between the two of them and maybe not, but they owed it to each other to find out.

Wynn pushed Claire into a chair after finding her washing dishes with one hand, the tiny baby in the other arm. "Where's Mrs. Matthews?"

"She has the day off, so she went to visit her sister."

"Want me to take the baby or wash the dishes?"

"Dishes, please." Claire sighed as Wynn filled the teapot and put it on the stove. She had a simple headband holding her light brown hair back from her face. "Bertie had to be at the diner this morning. Can you hand me that bottle off the counter? I tried to feed her a little while ago, and she wasn't ready for it."

"I thought the baby was temporary?" Wynn picked up the bottle, shook it a little and handed it to Claire.

"She is. Two more days. And she's the last for a while. I promised Joe that we'd keep the status quo here for three months after the baby is born. Ohhhh." Claire let out a long, drawn-out half laugh, half groan.

Wynn turned the water off. "Claire, was that a contraction?"

"Yeah, I've been having Braxton Hicks for a month. I'm fine—I've just been on my feet all morning. The baby's not due for a couple more weeks." She looked up as Wynn placed a steaming cup of herbal tea on the side table. "Thanks. So Latham looked a little pale when he came in for Pop the other night after he tutored the kids."

Heart skittering ahead of itself, Wynn began picking up toys from the floor, placing them in the big wicker baskets on either side of the fireplace. "That's strange."

Claire looked at her with knowing eyes. "I thought so. Is there something going on with you two?"

"No." Wynn's cheeks flushed hot as she

thought about the toe-tingling kiss they'd shared at the cottage two nights ago and the charged conversation yesterday in her mom's office.

Luckily, Claire's eyes were on the baby in her lap. "Still, it must be weird seeing him again after all these years. You, Joe, Ash and Latham were all pretty tight, right?" She sucked in a breath. "Oh wow, these contractions are definitely stronger than they were yesterday."

"It is weird. We're all grown up now, and I'm honestly not sure I know what to do with it all." Wynn picked up the last toy and sat beside Claire on the couch, watching her carefully. Wynn knew next to nothing about labor, but Claire's contractions didn't seem to be the mild Braxton Hicks ones that she'd read about in the books. "Have those been hurting like that all morning?"

"Yeah. My back is killing me, too." Claire lifted the baby to her shoulder and began patting the tiny back, no wider than her hand. Claire paused midpat, her face going white. "Wynn, is it—do you think—it's possible I might be in labor?"

Wynn tried not to laugh. After all, this would be her in a few months. "I think so.

If my timing is right, your contractions are about five minutes apart."

Claire tried to get off the sofa and failed, wailing in frustration. "How am I going to have a baby if I can't even get off the couch?"

Wynn slid the baby from Claire's arms into her own and handed Claire her phone. "Call Joe."

Wynn placed the sleeping baby into the cradle in the corner and tried not to listen to the conversation between her brother and his wife. Even so, it was impossible not to hear her brother's impatient tone as he answered the phone and how his voice softened when he realized it was Claire.

"Babe, don't panic." Claire looked at Wynn and rolled her eyes up as a shout came through the phone. "Joe, it's time to go to the hospital. I've been having contractions all morning and they're getting close to being five minutes apart."

Claire laughed then winced, pressing her taut belly. "Joe, listen to me. Stop yelling and get me to the hospital."

She hung up the phone and closed her eyes. "We should be hearing sirens in about a minute and a half, the way he drives."

"What can I do?"

"My bag is beside the door to the bedroom. I have a plan in place for the kids, but my plan involves Bertie and Mrs. Matthews." Claire sat straight up on the couch. "I can't have a baby today. I have seven—eight—children to take care of."

Wynn found Claire's bag in the bedroom just as, true to Claire's prediction, she heard her brother's police siren in the distance. She went back into the kitchen living area. "I had a background check so I could babysit Levi for Jordan, so I've got this. Just tell me where they are."

"The little ones are at preschool. Penny and Matthew are at the elementary school. Amelia, Aleecya and Jackson are at the upper school. All the pickup times and where they all are is written on the calendar on the fridge. The keys to my van are hanging by the back door."

"Don't worry. I'll take care of everything here." The wail of Joe's police siren was getting closer. "I promise."

Joe slammed the kitchen door open, whipping off his silver aviators. "Claire?"

She lifted a hand. "Right here."

He hauled her to her feet and pulled her close, a tender look in his ice-blue eyes. "Baby, we've got to go. I called ahead. They're going to be waiting for us. It's lights and siren all the way."

"Sounds fun." Claire groaned and blew out a long, slow breath.

"The kids?"

Through gritted teeth, Claire said, "Wynn's got the command."

Joe turned to Wynn. "Don't panic. Everything will go fine. Just follow the chart. I'll get Mom to help you."

As he rushed Claire out the door, he met her eyes. "Thanks, sis. I'll keep you posted."

Wynn closed the door behind him and leaned against it. Claire and Joe were in this together, and when Claire called, Joe dropped everything to come to her. His tender care of his wife just illuminated the fact that Wynn was doing this all on her own.

She had her mom and her siblings and even, on some level, Latham. The blessing of those relationships did not escape her, but she'd be lying if she didn't admit to a little twinge of envy at her brothers' rock-solid relationships.

The baby in the cradle whimpered, her tiny cries like the mew of a cat. She'd had a bottle. Now what?

Whimpers turned to a wail, and Wynn wanted to join in. What kind of madness had she just volunteered for?

Chapter Eight

Wynn sat at Claire's kitchen island with the chart detailing where the kids were and when to pick them up, making her battle plan. Claire had the schedules color coded and separated by days of the week. Apparently picking them up at school wasn't the end of it. There were doctor's appointments, therapy appointments, caseworker visits and visits with the biological family.

She turned to baby Maureen, who was snuggled into a bouncy seat in the middle of the island in front of Wynn. Dark blue eyes blinked at her. "Auntie Wynn is not prepared for this, little one."

Changing Maureen's diaper, she took a second to marvel at the tiny fingers and toes and knees. They were precious down to the itty-bitty fingernails. Looking at this baby's fingers reminded her of her own baby, uncurling minuscule fingers inside her. It was the most amazing thing she had ever seen. And in a few short months—very few now—she would be changing her own baby's diaper.

Her stomach churned at the thought. She knew where they would be living right after the baby's birth, of course, but she still had no idea what she would do to make a living for them. She had a law degree and she'd passed the bar exam, but she hadn't practiced, instead going straight to Washington, DC. Her mom kept telling her that God had a plan. If He did, she wished He would fill her in on the details. She wasn't very good at trusting that things would work out. And maybe that was the point?

She was saying, *God, I want a map of my future, right now.* Maybe God was saying, *Learn to wait on My timing.*

It took her three tries to get all the snaps on the baby's onesie—or was this a sleeper?—snapped correctly. By the time she finished, she had a fine sheen of perspiration on her forehead and felt like an imbecile.

She strapped the infant into the car seat—another feat for which she needed an engineering degree—and was just picking her up when she heard a knock. She walked into the kitchen, expecting to see her mom at the door, but instead, when she pulled it open, Latham stood on the other side.

Her stomach did one crazy flip at the sight of him standing there. He had sawdust on his cheek, and her fingers itched to brush it away. She opened the door wider. "Hey, what are you doing here?"

"Joe called me. Your mom had an emergency at the diner—a dishwasher or something. I'm fuzzy on the details. Jordan has clients back-to-back all day. Mrs. Matthews is on her way back from her sister's, but it will be tonight before she gets here."

"Okay, that's fine. It's just one day, right?" Surely she could handle this for one day. Actually, she wasn't sure at all. She'd needed electrolytes after a simple diaper change.

"I only had one job this morning, so I'm free until class tonight." He nodded at the infant car seat on her arm. "Where are you headed?"

"Preschool pickup. Then back here for two hours while the little ones nap, then carpool again for the older kids. First the elementary school for Penny and Matthew and then the upper school for Amelia and the other two, brother and sister…" She was usually so good with names. It was a required skill in Washington. She snapped her fingers as it came to her. "Aleecya and Jackson."

"Impressive. Can I ride shotgun?"

It was just one day, and diaper bags and preschool carpool would be her life in a few months. She would have to learn to handle it because there wouldn't be anyone else to handle it for her. "*Please* ride shotgun."

In Claire's enormous van, Wynn snapped the baby's car seat into position, dropped the diaper bag under the seat and noticed a small cooler between the two front seats. "Any idea what that cooler is for?"

"Maybe drinks and snacks to keep the kids happy in the car?"

Brilliant. "Good thought. I'll run back in and see if I can find some sippy cups."

In the refrigerator, she found the cups filled and color coded in the same colors as the chart. Her sister-in-law was a master of organization, but then she would have to be with so many children and schedules to manage. Wynn was going to have to take lessons.

Back in the van, Wynn tossed the cups into the cooler with the icepack she'd retrieved from the refrigerator and a few random snack bags. She started the engine, took a deep breath and looked at her unlikely partner for the day. Meeting his eyes, she felt her stomach do another insane flip that, once again, had nothing to do with the chaos of tasks facing her.

Latham smiled. "Here's to adventures."

She snorted a laugh. "*No.* No adventures. Calm, that's what we're after."

He laughed, too, as he put on his seat belt. She reached over and rubbed the sawdust off his cheek with her thumb, and when he met her eyes, she wished that things were different, that she was the kind of person whom he should be interested in.

But she wasn't.

Forty-five minutes later, Latham sighed in relief when Wynn pulled into the van's parking spot beside the house at Red Hill Farm. Navigating even these country roads in this enormous van that happened to be full of squalling children was not an easy task. Thirty minutes of crying, starting when the preschool teachers buckled the two babies into their respective seats and they looked to the front only to realize that the inhabitants of the van were not whom they expected. Mama Claire wasn't in the driver's seat, and that was *not* okay with them.

Two minutes from the farm, the wails had turned to snivels, and sixty seconds from home, blessed silence had fallen as the two very unhappy toddlers drifted into exhausted sleep.

He very much could use a nap himself at this moment.

Wynn pushed the gearshift into place and sat back with a sigh. "Wow. That was intense."

Latham laughed softly. "No kidding. Do you want to take them inside?"

"Not a chance." She rolled the windows down and turned off the ignition. As she did, the baby in the carrier, who had slept through the entire debacle, began to squirm, eyes still closed.

"Uh-oh." Latham raised an eyebrow. "This plan may be short-lived."

Wynn reached behind her and snagged the diaper bag. "If you can get Maureen, I have a bottle in here somewhere."

Latham walked back to the seat where the baby's carrier was locked in. He pushed back the handle and unbuckled the straps, wondering at the tiny little body that they protected. She was still sleeping, but her mouth was working, and he knew it wouldn't be long before she, too, would be shouting her displeasure.

He lifted her out of the seat. Her whole

body fit in one of his wide, rough hands, and for the first time in his life, he wished that they were softer.

Easing into the seat, he held the baby out to Wynn, who shook her head and handed him the bottle.

"It's okay, I'm good. You can feed her."

He raised a skeptical eyebrow but stuck the bottle in the baby's mouth. She grabbed on with a zeal that was surprising. He grinned down at the diminutive face. "She's pretty cool to be so little."

Wynn leaned back in her seat. "Claire said she was born a month early. The foster parents who will have her for the long term couldn't take her just yet, so she came here for a week first as an emergency placement."

Maureen finished sucking down the bottle and, when he lifted her to his shoulder, let out a decidedly unladylike burp. A laugh rumbled out of his chest. He reached down for the lever for his seat and eased it back, letting the baby lie on his chest. Her breath hitched out in a tiny sigh, and his heart melted a little.

"I think you have a knack." Wynn's voice was soft in the quiet car. "I'm not nearly as easy with her as you are."

"When's your baby due?" As soon as the words were out, he regretted them.

A guarded look came over her face as her hand curved protectively around her still small baby bump, but she answered him. "I'm getting close to halfway. I have twenty more weeks or so to go."

The baby in his arms stirred, and he patted her until she settled again. "Have you thought of a name for her?"

Wynn smiled softly, relaxing into her seat. "Maybe Eleanor, or Margaret. Something feminine, but strong."

"Like you."

She cut her eyes at him. "My mom named me Edwynna and called me Eddy until I was old enough to choose my own name. I climbed trees and skipped rocks and played in the mud. Not exactly feminine."

"You had an awesome childhood. Everyone wanted their mom to be like Bertie." He grinned. Like just about every man in Red Hill Springs, he'd had a crush on Bertie Sheehan for as long as he could remember.

"I did. My mom's amazing. She didn't want me or Jules to ever be overlooked just for being female. I didn't appreciate it as a kid but I can now, especially since I know I'm carrying a daughter."

He and Wynn weren't alone sitting here in the driveway at Red Hill Farm, not even close. Across the backyard, Jordan was in the arena doing a therapy session with several kids on horseback, and she had three volunteers working with her. A couple of parents watched from the fence line. Even so, the van felt like it was insulated from the real world. Maybe it was that feeling that gave him the courage to ask, "Were you happy in Washington before...you know, you came home?"

Wynn turned wide blue eyes to his. "Was I happy? I don't know—what does that even mean?"

He lifted one shoulder in a slight shrug. "I don't know. It's just a question."

"I was busy." Her voice dropped. "I think sometimes maybe I confused busyness with happiness. What about you? Are you happy with your life?"

I would be if you were in it. The words came, uncalled, into his mind. He pushed the thought away and tried to answer her question. "I'm content, I guess. I like that my roots are in Red Hill Springs and I've chosen to live here."

He looked away from her eyes that seemed to see so much, but he told her the truth, because if anyone could understand the way he felt, Wynn could. "I had dreams for my life, but things changed and here I am."

Her soft voice washed over him. "Things like your gran died and Pop needed you?"

"Yes." He shifted in the seat, and he wasn't sure if he was uncomfortable from sitting or uncomfortable with the conversation. "I wanted to teach full-time. It wasn't my plan to be a carpenter, but I have the skills and it gives me the freedom to set my own schedule, which is important to me right now."

"You're so good at what you do, it never occurred to me that it wasn't what you wanted to do." She reached out with one hand, her fingers lacing with his in a completely unconscious gesture.

He looked at their joined hands, hers soft and pale, his rough and work-hardened. His other hand held the baby to his chest. "I don't resent having to change my plans for my life. This sounds really cliché or cheesy or something, but it's my honor to be with Pop. He and Gran raised me, and I guess I just figure it's my turn to take care of him. I have a feeling that when your baby comes, you won't think about the circumstances anymore, you'll just know what a gift she is."

Her eyes, when she looked up, were glossy. "I wish things were different, Latham. I wish—" One of the toddlers in the back woke up with a gasp and looked around with wild, questioning eyes.

Wynn jumped up, looking relieved that she didn't have to finish that sentence.

"Looks like rest time is over. Hey, little man, you ready to go in and get a cookie?" She unbuckled the seat and lifted the little boy into her arms. "I'm going to take him in for a diaper change and cookie. You good here?"

"Yeah." He watched as she bounced the little boy across the yard. He kicked up a fuss, but Wynn persisted, stopping and kissing his belly. Latham laughed himself when she finally got a smile to appear on that small cross face.

He had no idea what she'd been about to say, but he wished things were different, too.

He'd never wished that more than he did right now.

Wynn peeked around the door to Claire's birthing suite. It wasn't like any room she'd ever seen, the decor less like a hospital and more like a living room. She knocked softly, and her sister-in-law looked up with a smile. "Come in."

"Mrs. Matthews got back about an hour ago and Mom came to help her put the children to bed." And just in time, too. Wynn felt like a wrung-out dishrag after all those hours with Claire and Joe's eight—now nine—kids. She took a few steps forward and tried to see into the blanket-wrapped bundle in Claire's arms. "No one would tell me if you had a boy or a girl."

Claire looked up at Joe, standing beside her. "Should we tell her?"

"Tell me!"

Joe grinned and nudged his thirteen-year-old daughter, Amelia, on his other side. "You tell her."

"It's a girl. Your baby's gonna have a girl cousin just her age." Amelia beamed. "I bet they're close, like sisters."

Wynn's breath caught in her throat. Amelia didn't mean anything, but the words felt like plans, and plans felt really big and really final. Making decisions about her future and the weight of it all sometimes threatened to suffocate her.

But then, Claire turned the little bundle to reveal a tiny red, wrinkled face—and Wynn could breathe again. "Oh, guys, she's beautiful."

Joe kissed his wife on the forehead. "Claire was a champ. You want to hold her?"

"Oh, no. I can't stay—oh—oh, wow." Wynn

closed her arms around the baby as Joe handed her over and she looked down into the surprisingly alert eyes of her newest niece, tears gathering in her own. "Did you decide what to name her?"

"Her name is Abigail Frances."

She looked for Joe through the haze of tears. "After Dad?"

He nodded, swallowing hard himself. "We decided as soon as we knew we were having a baby that, boy or girl, our baby would be named after Dad. We're calling her Frankie."

Wynn laughed. "Of course you are. He would be so proud of you, Joe. *I'm* proud of you."

With a kiss on the head of the sweet baby girl, she passed Frankie back to him. "I'm not going to stay. I know you're all tired. Reinforcements have arrived for the children, but if you need anything tomorrow, please let me help."

She hugged Amelia and walked out the door, closing it behind her. The tears that she'd been holding back coursed down her cheeks, a sob catching in her throat. She had to get out of here.

She was so overwhelmed with the *namelessness* of what was rushing in at her, she couldn't breathe.

Waiting for the elevator, she swiped the tears off her cheeks and rubbed the mascara out from under her eyes. When the doors opened, Latham stood there, a large takeout bag from a local restaurant in his hands. He took one look at her face and took her by the arm. "What's wrong?"

His face swam before her. "I'm fine. I just need to go."

He searched her face, his deep brown eyes filled with concern. "Wait here. I'm just gonna drop this food with Joe and I'll be right back. Promise me you'll wait."

The sobs were coming again, welling into the back of her throat, and she nodded, unable to speak for fear of completely breaking down. She leaned against the wall, her hand across her eyes.

He was back in just a moment and put his arm around her, leading her into the elevator. She buried her head in his chest and he didn't speak, just held her close, until they got outside the hospital.

He sat her on a bench. "Don't move. I'll be right back."

She didn't know where he thought she would go. She couldn't even see.

He came back a few seconds later with a

noncaffeinated soda. "Drink. I don't like how pale you are."

She took a few sips of the soda and a few deep breaths, trying to get her mind around why she was so upset. "Thanks. I thought you had class tonight."

"I did. It's over. Want to talk about what's bothering you?"

She shot him a look. "Not really. I think I'm just—so tired."

"It was a long day."

"It's not that. Or maybe I'm tired because of that, and the other stuff just bubbled to the surface." She looked at him, and her throat clogged again. "I don't know what I'm doing."

He put his arm around her and leaned back on the bench. She relaxed into the embrace, taking that little bit of comfort, even though she knew she shouldn't, not with the way things were. "Tell me what you're thinking. Maybe talking it through out loud will help."

She stared at the small pond in front of the hospital, where ducks swam serenely. "They're such a unit. It's so obvious when you're around them."

A furrow formed between his brows. "Joe and Claire?"

"All of them. I'm so happy for them, Latham. You understand that, right?"

"Of course."

"They named the baby after my dad." The tears started again. "What is wrong with me?"

"Nothing's wrong with you. It's perfectly normal to be emotional about a new addition in the family." He paused. "And it's perfectly normal that it brings up questions and thoughts about your own upcoming addition to the family."

"I don't want to do this by myself," she whispered, watching the ducks waddle out of the pond and settle to sleep on the bank. "I can feel her, you know."

"Your baby?"

"I can feel her moving. At first, it felt like a butterfly, but now I feel her moving and kicking. She's an actual human being, Latham, and I'm in charge of her happiness. It's terrifying. And when I see Joe and Claire and Amelia surrounding that little baby up there with love and security, I think I'm doing it wrong."

He turned her to face him. "Listen to me, Wynn. This is important. She will feel secure because her security will be you. And you'll have all of us as backup, just like Claire and Joe do. They don't parent alone, and you don't have to either."

Something eased inside at his words. "You're really annoying, you know that?"

A surprised laugh shot out. "I've been told that before." He was silent for a minute, and when she looked up at him, she couldn't read the expression on his face. Finally, he said, "I'll always have your back, Wynn."

"You always have." She said it lightly, but the words rocked her. "I have to go. Thanks for tonight, Latham."

She stood and started toward her car. He'd had her back every time one of her brothers tried to play tricks on her. Every time someone picked on her at school. Every time.

Every time she'd needed him, he'd been there.

Was it any wonder she'd fallen in love with him once? She glanced back at him. He was sitting in the same place, his elbows braced on his knees, head down, almost like he was praying.

She wished she had the freedom to fall in love with him again.

Chapter Nine

Mayor Chip Campbell held the chair out for Wynn and she slid into place at the table. "I'm glad you could join me, Wynn. I've been following your career with interest. I have to say, I was surprised when you came home a few months ago."

She looked up as Lanna, her mom's second in command at the diner, stopped by with a pitcher of water. "Thanks."

"I heard about Claire and Joe's new baby, named after your dad. It's just the sweetest." Lanna filled the mayor's glass and asked, "Okay, you folks ready to order?"

Mayor Campbell motioned for Wynn to go first.

"I want the Belgian waffle with bacon on the side." She was starving and had decided at home while she was debating on what to wear to breakfast with the mayor that being herself was the best course of action. She'd chosen jeans and a cute top and was going to order exactly what she wanted.

"With berries and whip?" Lanna had her pencil poised over her pad, even though Wynn well knew that she didn't need the pencil or the pad.

"Definitely." There weren't that many advantages to being pregnant, other than the baby at the end of it, but having an excuse to eat what you wanted without feeling guilty was one of them. After her emotional night last night, she wanted comfort food, the food she'd grown up with at the Hilltop Café.

Mayor Campbell seemed torn. "I should be having oatmeal and berries, but I think I'm going to go with blueberry pancakes. I just can't resist the temptation."

"Good choice, Mr. Mayor." Lanna took their menus. "Coffee?"

The mayor nodded. "Wynn?"

"None for me, thanks. I'll stick with water," she said as Lanna reached behind her for the coffeepot.

Chip stirred sugar into the coffee Lanna poured into his mug. "I'm happy you've gotten to spend some time in Red Hill Springs. Your mother has missed you."

"I've missed being here. More than I realized." She said the words, a little shocked that they were true. She'd been so focused on leaving Washington, DC, that she hadn't processed what coming home really meant to her.

"And you're planning to stay? I heard you're renovating the cottage at Red Hill Farm."

Wynn took a sip of her water and replaced her glass on the table, giving herself a second to think. In the end, she asked lightly, "Does anything happen in Red Hill Springs without your hearing about it?"

He chuckled as Lanna slid his pancakes onto the table, along with a small pitcher of warm maple syrup. "Not much, no. I like to think I have my finger on the pulse of the town, as they say."

Lanna came back a minute later with Wynn's order, sliding it into place in front of Wynn. "Y'all let me know if you need anything, okay?"

Chip took a bite of his pancakes and rolled his eyes back in his head. Wynn's mom's pancakes were the best in the state.

"I don't know why I ever order anything else. So...you *are* planning to stay in the area?"

"To be honest, I'm not sure about the long

term, sir. I don't have any other plans at the moment." She took a deep breath. "Well, other than to have a baby."

He glanced up in surprise, his fork suspended in midair. "Really?"

She willed herself not to blush. "Yes. A baby girl. Due in a few months."

Behind his glasses, the mayor's dark brown eyes were sharply direct on hers. "And the father?"

"Not in the picture." She took a sip of water as the heat crept up her neck.

"I see." The mayor abruptly noticed his empty fork was still hanging in the air and stabbed a bite of pancakes.

She wondered if he did, indeed, see, or if he was racking his brain trying to figure a way out of breakfast with her.

He didn't leave her wondering very long. "So, Charlie McCurdy decided last week that he's too old for—well, he decided to retire from the city council, effective at the end of the month. He has ten months left in his term. I'm hoping you'll consider filling it."

Wynn blinked. Opened her mouth. Blinked again. "You want me to be on the city council?"

His mouth full, Chip nodded.

She put her fork down. "I don't know what to say."

He lifted a shoulder and his coffee cup. "You don't have to say anything now, if you want to think about it. I need to know by the end of next week, though, so I can go to my second choice."

She was his first choice? That was unexpected...and flattering. But Chip had obviously been surprised by her pregnancy. Would he have asked her if he knew before he was sitting across the table from her?

Stomach churning, she had to ask before she could even think about taking the appointment. "Mayor Campbell, I'm so honored, but do you need to rethink your offer? My pregnancy will be showing soon."

He took another bite of his pancakes and chewed, not looking concerned at all. When he swallowed, he took a swig of coffee before he leaned back in his seat and tossed his napkin on the table. "Wynn, I've made it my policy not to let personal issues limit my political choices. You're a brilliant strategist, according to several people I talked to in Washington. You know Red Hill Springs, and even more important, you care what happens here."

She slid her fingers into her hair, scratched

her head and studied him in honest disbelief. She wanted to know whom he talked to in Washington, but that wasn't a question she could ask, at least not now. "I'm floored. And really so honored that you would think of me."

He pushed away from the table. "Red Hill Springs is a small town. City council's not a Senate seat, but it'll be good experience for you. I won't be mayor forever."

Wynn's mouth dropped open as Chip picked up the check and patted her hand. Did he just suggest that she run for mayor when his term was up?

"I'll look forward to hearing from you, Wynn." He stopped, then smiled. "Congratulations on the baby."

She found her voice. "Yes, sir."

As he paid the check and left the restaurant, she stared at the wall.

Well, that was not what she expected. She'd thought they would be talking about mutual acquaintances and state politics. Instead, he'd offered her a job. If she took the job, it would mean staying in Red Hill Springs, probably for the long term. A decision she hadn't been planning to make by the end of next week.

So now what did she do?

* * *

That afternoon at Red Hill Farm, Latham rounded his truck and pulled down the tailgate. His subcontractors had finished the work on the outside of the cottage. The siding, in pearl gray, had been installed, and he was here for the finish work—hanging the porch swings and shutters, and painting the front door. Which he would do if he could ever get Wynn to make up her mind on the color.

The farm, as usual, was teeming with action. He brought Pop and Aunt Mae with him today because Pop insisted that the kids needed him to help with their math homework. He brought Aunt Mae because she wasn't being left behind at the house while Pop was out doing things.

His seventy-two-year-old aunt was currently keeping an eye on the toddlers who were racing their riding toys in the ballroom. She was also folding laundry as fast as Mrs. Matthews could do it because it piled up quickly with seven kids. To be honest, Latham had never seen such a huge pile of dirty laundry, and Claire had been in the hospital only one day.

Pop was ensconced at the kitchen island with the teenagers, doing their math homework and calling out spelling words to Penny.

The kids really responded to his easygoing, funny personality. Maybe it was that he treated them like they were the most special kids in the world.

He'd always treated Latham like that, too.

Wynn came out the back door wearing tiny baby Maureen in some wrap thing that looked like a papoose. She called across the yard. "Hey, can I help?"

Latham raised an eyebrow. "I think you have your hands full enough."

He shouldered the stained board-and-batten shutters and started for the cottage, as she clambered down the stairs.

She called after him. "I bought a couple more paint colors to test on the door."

"Of course you did." This was not a surprise. There were already at least ten test paint colors in the house, waiting to be tried on the door.

She was at his heels as he rounded the pond. "I left them on the porch. We're going to try them today, yes?"

He couldn't turn around because he would whack her in the face with the shutters, but he grinned. She was relentless when it came to something she wanted. That was probably what made her good at her job in Washington. She wouldn't let up until whoever she was arguing with just gave in.

"Latham." There was a warning tone in her voice.

Latham didn't answer, and he heard her footsteps stop. He took a couple of more steps and swung around, the shutters turning with him. "Yes, we're going to try the colors. Happy?"

"Yes." She smiled at him and—seriously, he'd heard this before, but didn't believe it was real—his heart stopped for a second. She was standing there on the path, just a girl in jeans and a T-shirt, her arms curved protectively around the baby she was holding. He shook his head. Why this girl? Why could he not just get over her?

She cocked her head. "Do you think sea green would be better than mint? Because I saw one at the store and I thought about it. There was also a peach that might be really pretty with the gray siding."

He turned back toward the cottage and walked away from her. If he didn't get the door painted soon, they'd have half the paint colors at the home improvement store in swatches on the front door.

Praying for patience, he leaned the cedar-wood shutters against the porch rail at the cottage and plugged his drill into the outdoor plug. He'd predrilled the holes in the siding planks, so if he'd measured right...he hoisted the shutter up and screwed it to the wall, stepped on a small ladder and drilled the top screws in.

Aware that Wynn was watching him from a safe distance, he had all four wood shutters on the house in no time. He took a step back. "What do you think?"

She walked closer, one hand around the baby, the other reaching out to touch the natural wood he'd sanded and stained. "I love it. The shutters look amazing. I love the natural wood with the gray siding and the white trim. It's perfect."

"I have a couple more things to do and then we'll talk about the paint color, okay?"

"Thank you. I'm so excited. I can't wait to move in! I love my mom, but there's such a thing as too much togetherness."

He looked over at the main house. "Speaking of your mom..."

She whirled around and then back, her eyes sparkling. "The cavalry has arrived. I'm going to go hand Maureen off and see how Pop and Aunt Mae are holding up, and then I'll be back to pick a paint color!"

Laughing, he pushed the door open to the

cottage. The contractors had finished up the loft area. It wasn't huge, but there was a window and it looked out over the pond. It would be a great little studio. He would install the railing tomorrow. He was using the natural wood again, with hog wire. It would be modern and clean and still keep the rustic feel of the house. He couldn't wait to see it complete, but for today, he was hanging the shutters and the porch swings.

After their conversation at the hospital, he'd stayed up late in his workshop last night finishing the custom porch swings so he could surprise her today. She'd been more open than ever about how she felt about having a baby and being a single mom.

He could understand the fear and even the frustration of having to change your life so suddenly, even if you really wanted to. It was the equivalent of driving toward a destination, playing your tunes and rocking along and suddenly you realize you've made a wrong turn and there's no way to get back to the path you were on. Maybe at some point you realize where this path leads is better, or ends up at somewhere awesome, but that doesn't take away the feelings you have about changing the planned destination.

He finished screwing the large eyebolts

into the ceiling of the porch and lifted one end of the swing and hooked it on before repeating the action on the other side. With a gentle push, he tested it out.

Glancing up to see if Wynn was still at the house, he quickly hung the other swing. He stepped back from the porch to look. The natural wood columns and shutters were perfect, and the swings, handmade in his shop, looked great.

Would Wynn rock her baby in these swings? He hoped so. He hoped she would stay, and then wondered, Would it feel like a cop-out to her if she did?

He wanted what was best for her, and he wasn't the one who could decide that. He turned toward the main house and saw her coming down the path, a paintbrush in her hand, her blond hair shining in the sunlight.

No, he wasn't the one who could decide if she would stay, but he would do anything in his power to make it hard for her to go.

Wynn took a step back. She'd picked her top three paint colors. She just wasn't sure. "I think maybe we should try that other one."

Latham picked up the two small cans. "*Mint Soufflé* or *Mint Julep*? They're not *at all* the same. I mean, the difference is subtle, but you would definitely be making a mistake if you chose the wrong one."

She brushed the last stroke of the color she'd just tried, *Mint Ice Cream*. "I know, right?"

She heard his chuckle and stopped. "Oh, I get it. That was sarcasm." She took a couple of steps toward him. "I wouldn't mess with a lady with a paintbrush."

He leaned against the wall. "Oh yeah? What are you going to—Wynn!" He spluttered as she tapped him on the nose with the brush, cutting him off.

Tilting her head, she looked up at him. "I have to say, I like the color. Mint Ice Cream, it is."

"Glad we finally picked a color." He rubbed the paint off his nose.

She tapped the brush on his cheek, leaving another paint smudge. She beamed at him. "Yep, I like that one. Just wanted to make sure."

Whisking her into his arms, he started for the pond, his long stride eating up the distance. He shrugged. "You know, Wynn, if I have to take a bath, I think it's only fair that you do, too."

She shrieked. "No! Latham, no! That pond is fifty-something degrees even in the summer. You can't throw me in there! It's February. I'll freeze!"

When he just smiled down at her and kept walking, she pulled out the big guns. "I'm pregnant! You can't throw a pregnant lady!"

"Wanna bet? You're really not that heavy!" He started laughing and nearly dropped her.

In desperation, she used her last weapon. "The baby's kicking!"

Latham went still, with her in his arms. She was freaking out, and he hadn't even broken a sweat.

He looked down at her. "What did you say?"

Wynn kept her eyes on his. She couldn't have looked away if she wanted to, not with that intense gaze on hers. "I said, the baby's moving. You can feel it, I think, if you want to."

Latham gently set her feet down on the grass. "Are you sure it's really okay?"

"Yes, I'm sure." She was still tucked into the curve of his arm, so she took his other hand. She closed her eyes, waiting. *There.* She placed his hand right over where the little stinker's foot just kicked her. "Over just a little bit."

His big hand, rough and gentle, slid across her belly under hers, and she had to remind herself to breathe. The baby kicked again. "There. Did you feel it?"

"Wynn," he said, his voice quiet. "It's a baby."

It was crazy and weird and somehow perfect, to have this little life growing inside her. She nodded. "Yeah, she's really there. Isn't that just the coolest thing?"

The look of wonder in his eyes nearly undid her. She took a couple of steps away, and he tugged her back, scooping her into his arms again. "Break's over. Now you're going in the pond."

"What? No!" She gave him her sternest face. "Latham, you can't throw me in the pond."

"Oh, all right." He set her on the ground and dusted a kiss across her lips. "Come on, Mama, let's go paint your door."

Wynn took a couple of steps after him as he walked away, a paintbrush sticking out of his back pocket. He was so effortlessly manly, not like the men she'd known in Washington at all.

She stopped. *No.* This was pregnancy hormones talking, not feelings. *Right?*

He turned around. "Coming?"

She followed him onto the porch, heart slamming in her chest. *No, no, no, no.* It was not possible for her to be falling for Latham Grant again.

Not possible at all.

Chapter Ten

Latham snagged the basketball out of the air and dribbled down the concrete pad at Red Hill Farm to the other end for a layup. He caught the rebound and bounced it back to Joe, who dribbled slowly toward the center-line. The sky was clear and blue—a warm gift of a winter's day with just enough of a breeze to be amazing.

"You're a little bit off today." He stepped into Joe's personal space, arms up, determined not to let him get a shot off.

"You try not sleeping for a week and see how well you play basketball." From the three-point line, Joe tossed the ball and it didn't even make it to the goal.

"Air ball." Latham scooped up the ball as it rolled down the court. "Dude, c'mon. I gotta work off all the chocolate cake Aunt Mae's been feeding me."

"Basketball isn't my sport. I'm definitely better at soccer." Joe halfheartedly waved his arms in front of Latham's face.

"Are you, though?" From the free throw line, Latham sunk his shot. "You've had newborns before. What gives?"

Joe picked up the rebound, dribbled. "My wife hadn't just had a baby. It's different, trust me. You should listen, given the fact that you're dating my sister. My *pregnant* sister."

Latham blocked the shot and stole the ball. Joe was built, but Latham probably had at least a couple of inches on him. He took it down the court and did another layup. "You're making this too easy. And I'm not dating your sister."

Joe grinned. "Maybe, but you want to."

Latham narrowed his eyes at his best friend from childhood before passing the ball to him with a shrug. "I guess that's fair."

Joe dribbled slowly, his back to Latham. "Claire and I both thought, we've got this. We know what we're doing. We've had ten kids in one house before—one more baby isn't that big a deal. *Wrong.* This kid never sleeps."

Joe took a shot, and this time it went in. "You have no idea."

Latham went after the rebound and dribbled the ball. He honestly hadn't thought about what it would be like after Wynn's baby was born. He should have, especially after he'd felt her move last week: one of the most unbelievably amazing moments of his life.

He let the ball drop and bounce back from one hand to the other, imagining himself walking the floor with a tiny screaming baby. He shrugged. It didn't seem like that big a thing.

"Are we going to play, or are we done?" Joe scowled at Latham from across the court. He didn't look like he was ready to play. He looked like he was ready for a nap.

"We're done." Latham stuck the ball under one arm and walked toward the house, his mind still on what Joe had said. He liked babies. He liked Wynn. It was no big deal.

And he was really getting ahead of himself. Wynn hadn't given him any indication that she wanted the same thing out of this relationship that he did. Other than kissing him back that one time. He grinned. There was that.

He tossed Joe the ball. "I've got a few things to do at the cottage. It's almost finished."

"Come get a drink first."

The little boy, Matthew, who'd helped

Latham measure the first day he'd come to check out the cottage came running up. "I finished my homework, Chief."

Joe ruffled the boy's hair. "Good job. I'll check your math when I come inside."

"Can I play?" The little boy was fairly vibrating with pent-up energy.

"Yes. Go." Joe laughed as Matthew gave a banshee yell and ran to meet the other kids on the play set. "To think I was worried that he would never talk to us. He's firmly entrenched in the family now."

"Stopped trying to escape every thirty seconds?"

Joe glanced back at Latham. "Oh yeah, I forgot he ran to the cottage that time. He's been so protective of Claire since we got home from the hospital, he's hardly left her side."

In the backyard, Pop was at his spot at the picnic table with one of the girls next to him. Joe nodded at them. "Penny loves Pop. She calls him her 'grandpa.'"

"He loves to come out here and be with the kids. I think it gives him a sense of purpose. He's been better, too. More engaged in life, if that makes sense."

"It does. I can see it when I talk to him.

Hang on, I'll be right back with a drink." Joe disappeared into the house.

Latham's Aunt Mae was sitting in one of the porch rockers with a tiny baby on her chest. She'd made herself an indispensable part of life the last two weeks that she'd been here. He was going to miss her when she had to go back to Michigan. He snagged the chair next to her. "Claire and Joe's baby?"

"Yes. The toddlers are sleeping, so I told Claire to go take a nap, that I would watch Frankie for her."

The baby was wrapped up like a mummy with a tiny cap on her head. Her eyes were closed, and she had long dainty lashes and a tiny pink mouth. She would fit in one of his hands. And he wondered, had he ever spent so much time thinking about babies?

The serene pond and the little cottage with fresh gray siding were just beyond the barn. Wynn was sitting on the porch steps, having an animated chat with one of the teenage girls. He chuckled to himself as she stood up and did some kind of weird dance and collapsed back to the porch, laughing with Aleecya.

Aunt Mae's voice interrupted his thoughts. "Robert looks like he's doing better today than he was last night."

Latham nodded. "He does seem better. He used to have episodes like that a lot more often, where he was agitated and nothing I did could calm him down. I think he's better in general since he's been coming here."

Mae rocked a few times. "I like being here, too. I like Red Hill Springs."

"You could move here," he said idly, his eyes returning to watch the kids play in the yard.

She didn't say anything for a long moment. "Well, I don't really have a reason to stay in Michigan, now that Larry's gone. The kids are at opposite ends of the country, and they could just as easily come and visit me here."

He slowly spun around, so he could see her. She was a petite woman, who at seventy-two looked more like she was fifty-two. "Are you saying you want to move in with us?"

His aunt shrugged, shifting the baby into a different position as she started squirming. "I could buy a little house somewhere nearby, but if I live at your house, it will free you up a lot more. I know you had to give up the work you wanted to do and it's been really hard for you to have friends. I'm sorry I couldn't do more to help you. Larry was sick for so long."

He couldn't let her feel guilty for something she had no control over. It wasn't fair.

"Aunt Mae, I don't regret missing anything to be with Pop."

"I know you don't, sweetheart. And I know you're lucky to have each other. I just thought I might be able to ease things for you, just a little bit. Plus, I miss my brother."

Latham took her free hand between both of his. "I would love to have you move into the ranch house but don't move here for me and Pop, move here because it's what's best for you."

She nodded. Her eyes, the exact brown of his, were shining. "That's what I'll do. It will take me some time to pack my things, but I plan to keep the house in Michigan so we can vacation there when it's too hot to breathe in Alabama."

"Perfect. Pop is going to be so happy." He hugged his aunt gingerly, as the baby's dark blue eyes blinked open, and kissed her on the cheek. "*I'm* happy."

"I'm happy, too, now that I have a plan." Aunt Mae stood up and bounced. No longer just squirming, Baby Frankie was fussing in earnest, her little pink mouth primping. "I think it's time to take her inside to Claire. Latham, thank you. I never thought at seventy-two that I'd be moving across the country and starting over, but I'm so excited. I can't wait to start my new life. And, young man, I think it's about time you started yours, too."

Latham sat back in the rocking chair. He wasn't sure what his aunt was talking about, but as he looked to the cabin, he saw Wynn grab the hand of the teenager she was talking to, then pull her up the steps and into the cottage. Would Wynn be a part of his new life, or was that just a silly dream that he should've let go of a long time ago?

Wynn dragged one of the boxes labeled Pots and Pans into the kitchen. Everything she owned had been in storage for the last few months. She didn't even remember what was in the boxes.

Aleecya lifted a stack of plates and began unwrapping them. "These are really pretty."

Wynn glanced over from the box she was opening. "I love those pale yellow plates. I bought one place setting every time I got paid for my whole first year working."

"That's so cool. Mama Claire said you went to college up north and then worked in Washington, DC." Aleecya put a stack of plates into the cabinet.

"I did." Wynn pulled out the deepest drawer

and put the pots she'd stacked on the counter into it.

"What was it like? I want to get away from here so bad." Aleecya's dark brown eyes were focused on far-away dreams, and Wynn had to work at not being a bubble-burster.

"I had a lot of dreams, and some of them came true." She stopped, a pot lid clasped against her chest, and tried to answer Aleecya's question. "It was cool, living in DC. There's a real sense that it's the place where things get done. It was exciting to be a part of it."

"I want to live in a big city. I want a job in one of those skyscrapers." Aleecya pulled brown paper off the plates, stacking them carefully onto the counter.

The last thing Wynn wanted to do was step on anyone's parenting toes, but Aleecya was waiting for her to say something. She took a deep breath. "There's some things you can do to make your dreams come true. Study hard. Participate in clubs and be a leader. Get a scholarship to college and then keep studying hard and being a leader there. That's what opens doors in the long run."

"I will, I promise." Aleecya put another stack of plates into the cabinet. "You're so cool. I hope I can be like you someday."

Wynn winced. "You mean, moving into a three-room cottage that my brother and sister-in-law own because I got pregnant and came home? I'm no role model, Aleecya."

The teenager's eyes went huge and dark and wary. And Wynn felt awful. She made herself relax and smile. "Here's the thing. *You* have your whole life ahead of you. Make plans. Don't let anyone stop you. You can do whatever you set your mind to."

Aleecya shrugged one shoulder. "I'm just a foster kid. I don't even know how to apply for scholarships and stuff like that. It's easy when you have parents who care about you."

When Wynn had seen that notice in the paper that the man she loved was engaged to someone else, she had literally felt her heart break. She felt a similar ache right now. Aleecya had stars in her eyes, but she didn't believe she had the power to reach them.

"Somewhere in one of these boxes, I have a notebook. When I get moved in, we'll start a dream planner for you. Not wishes. *Dreams.* And plans to make those dreams come true. You can do whatever you set your mind to." Wynn touched Aleecya's arm and willed her to believe in herself. Believe that she was meant to be so much more than just a foster kid. "I'll help you. I promise."

A soft knock at the door caught both of them off guard. Latham stepped through the opening. "Aleecya, Pop's ready to help you do your homework."

The teenager hesitated.

Wynn gave Aleecya a quick, fierce hug and flicked her thumb at the door. "Get out of here. Do some math. I'll see you soon."

"Thanks."

Wynn nodded. "Anytime."

When Aleecya was gone, Wynn picked up a stack of dishes and turned to put them in the cabinet. "How much of that did you hear?"

Latham ambled into the room. "Enough. You gave her good advice, but more important, you gave her hope."

She shook her head. "I'm not the person she needs to be looking up to."

He took the stack of bowls from the counter and put them on the cabinet shelf. "You don't have to be perfect, Wynn. You recognized you were going in a direction you didn't want to go and you were brave enough to correct your course. You're *exactly* the kind of person the girls need as a role model."

She stared at him for a moment, unmoving. Then picked up another stack of bowls and placed them in the cabinet. "It's nice of you to say that."

He leaned on one elbow on the counter, deceptively lazy. "I know success feels better than struggle, but I also know that people who fail and get up again and keep going—those are the people who succeed in the end. Those are the people who those kids up there need, because their lives aren't easy. They come from a hard place, and what they need to know is there are people who've walked that path before them. You're showing them there's a future for them."

"Yes, but what happened to them wasn't their fault. I did this to myself. I gambled my future on someone who didn't—" She broke off the thought and the words. "Look, I don't want to talk about this."

"Maybe you did this to yourself, but you're changing your life." He smiled, and at that moment, she could've kissed him. Or punched him. She wasn't sure which, but she was leaning toward punching him. "Am I? Or was I just forced to make changes?"

She let her hands drop to her sides.

He shook his head. "You're so frustrating to me. The person who you are hasn't changed. You're still the dreamer, the idealist, the passionate world-changer. You can still change the world—maybe not from Washington, DC—but I challenge you to find a group of people more deserving of their world being changed than those kids up there. And for that matter, a group of people who are more dedicated to changing the world than Joe and Claire." He glanced at his watch. "I gotta go. I have a job this afternoon."

"It's Saturday."

"Yes, it is. You're not the only person whose life didn't go according to plan. So deal with it." He was scowling at her, and she burst out laughing.

"So deal with it?"

"Yes." The scowl faded, replaced by a hint of his usual geniality. "I mean it."

"Oh, I know." She leaned into the box and pulled out the next item, wrapped in paper.

"I'm going to work." He started toward the door.

The scowl had lifted from his face, but his frustration troubled her. "I'll be here. I'm going to finish unpacking these boxes, and tomorrow I'm going to be upstairs in the studio. I can't wait."

She let him get to the door before she said, "Latham. I love my house. Thank you."

"No need."

As he left, he held the door open for seven-year-old Penny, who skipped in. Wynn didn't think she'd ever seen that child without a smile on her face. She was sweetness personified. "What's up, Shiny Penny?"

"Mama Claire said to tell you if you get hungry to come up for supper. One of the church ladies made a casserole."

"Church lady casserole. My favorite." Wynn smiled and popped open the next box.

"Are you going to come to church with us in the morning now that you live here?"

Wynn's stomach lurched. "Ah, I hadn't thought about it."

"Why not?"

If anyone had asked her, she would have never said that you shouldn't go to church unless you have your life together. Did you tell a seven-year-old that you weren't into going to church because you were starting to show and didn't want to be judged for your unplanned pregnancy?

Penny smiled and patted Wynn on the hand. "You can sit by me."

When Penny said it, it sounded simple. *Just sit by me.*

So, Wynn said yes.

Chapter Eleven

Wynn sat in her car outside the church, staring at the doors as people poured in from around town. Having just unpacked all her boxes from her apartment in DC, she'd thought surely she could find something to wear. For an hour, she'd tried things on and discarded them onto the floor.

Everything felt wrong. It didn't help that her stomach had apparently picked today to pop out. There was no hiding her condition now—but maybe that was for the best. She'd just lay it all out there, let them judge her.

She expected the whispers, the veiled insults, the barely hidden fingers pointing in her direction. After all, she'd left town to make something of herself and she'd come home in disgrace, with nothing to show for it except a failed romance and an unplanned pregnancy.

Why wouldn't they judge her? Hadn't she judged them for never leaving the small town they'd grown up in?

Her hands were white-knuckled on the steering wheel. All she had to do was put the car in gear and drive away. She had her hand on the gearshift, but then the door to the church opened. A small figure wearing a baby blue gingham dress with black Mary Janes and little white lace-edged socks stepped out and stood by the stairs.

Penny's sweet blue eyes lit up every time she saw a car turn into the parking lot, and her face fell every time she realized it wasn't Wynn.

Wynn took a deep breath. Everything in her wanted to run away, but that precious little girl on the porch steps was waiting for her. She might be willing to let herself down, but there was no way she was letting Penny down.

She stepped out of the car and smoothed down the navy blue swing dress she'd finally settled on this morning. With a stubborn set to her chin, she started for the front door of the church.

As she reached the steps, Penny met her at the bottom. "Hi, Aunt Wynn. I like your dress."

Wynn choked out a laugh. "Thanks, Penny. I like your dress, too."

The little girl's hand tucked into hers, Wynn entered the church. She was late, and it seemed like every eye turned to stare at her as she stood in the back of the church. Her heart slamming in her chest, she froze. Penny tugged on her hand, and whispered, "Come on, Aunt Wynn."

Penny led her to a pew, where her mom and Jules stood to let her in. It wasn't until she sat down that she realized she was surrounded by her family. Her brother Ash turned and winked at her. He was sitting in front of her with Jordan and Levi. Her brother Joe, and Claire, with a baby carrier wedged into the pew and most of their kids in the row beside them, were sitting behind her. A lump settled in her throat as they stood to sing the first hymn. Latham eased into place beside her and surreptitiously gave her clammy hand a squeeze. Her high school friend Molly, whom she hadn't seen since the morning she'd run out of the Hilltop, peeked through three rows of people and gave her a little wave.

Latham leaned in. "I hear there are doughnuts in the fellowship hall. Want to make a break for it?"

"Shh. Don't tempt me." She looked up

as the music started, tears gathering in her eyes as she sang the words to the song about God's faithfulness. These precious people who loved her were encircling her in a silent message to everyone in the church: this is our daughter, our sister, our aunt, our friend. She'd loved the Lord since she was a teenager, but she hadn't prayed in a long time. Somewhere along the way, she'd started having faith in politics, in powerful people, in her own ability. Her causes were righteous, but she was not. She didn't deserve the acceptance and love of the Lord. And yet, as the pastor began to speak, she realized that He offered it anyway.

She closed her eyes, letting the words of the sermon flow over her, and she prayed. The words came slowly and haltingly, her heart creaking open to Him like a door with a rusty hinge.

Father God, You've felt so far away from me, but the truth is that when I left my family, I left You, too. I acted like my prayers weren't important and my faith wasn't vital to the person I'd been raised to be. Please, Father, forgive me for my actions, for my unbelief. Forgive me for forgetting that I'm Your daughter.

That prodigal son thing—it's for real. I

wanted to come home and wasn't sure if I could. I wasn't sure what kind of welcome I'd receive, but it's been so much more than I deserve.

Thank you, God, for loving me enough to accept me, even though I'm flawed and broken, and for giving me a family who loves You enough to do the same.

I love You.

She opened her eyes, the room blurring through her tears. Latham held her hand again, gripping it tightly in his, not letting go.

Her future was uncertain. Maybe she would be in Red Hill Springs, maybe not, but the panicked feeling was starting to fade. She'd made a life for herself before, and she could do it again. This time, she had the love of her family and the love of her heavenly Father. She'd always had these things, but now she vowed to never forget them again.

On the other side of her, Penny snuggled in, and Wynn put her arm around the sweet seven-year-old. She also had the love and trust of some unbelievably special kids.

As the sermon wrapped up, the butterflies in her stomach intensified again. Knowing that God loved her and forgave her still didn't mean the church people would. She glanced down the row and toward the door in the back of the sanctuary. Could she slip out before anyone noticed? Not without making a scene shoving past everyone and…being noticed.

The final hymn played and Wynn sang along, every muscle tensed and waiting. When she was in middle school, there was this one kid who always picked on her. When it happened, her brothers would appear, flanking her with their strength and support. Joe was shorter, but he was a wall. And Ash, on the other side, could disarm anyone with his dimpled smile. She'd always felt safe with them on either side of her.

When the breakup with the congressman happened, she'd been alone and she'd *felt* alone. She didn't feel alone now. She was anxious, but she had her family around her. She would be okay.

As soon as the hymn ended, Latham leaned in. "I need to help Aunt Mae get Pop out before he gets confused. I'll see you later?"

His hand was warm and firm on the small of her back, somehow feeling absolutely perfect there. Wynn looked up to find his beautiful brown eyes on hers. She nodded. "Yes, go. I'll be fine."

He slipped out of the pew, and she followed him with her eyes. As people started milling around, her friend Molly, her hair curled into perfect waves, made a beeline for her, leaning over the pew to give Wynn a hug. "Hey, girl, it's so good to see you in church."

"Thanks. It's, um, been a while." Wynn tried a laugh, but it fell flat as, from the corner of her eye, she saw one of her mother's friends pointing to her and whispering to her companion.

"Oh, listen, I didn't come for months after my mom died. I just couldn't face it. It's okay. I think people understand sometimes we need our space. If they don't, they should." Molly looked across the room and waved at her husband. "Look, there's James. I hope he remembers our kids are in the nursery."

"I haven't seen him since graduation. He looks exactly the same." Molly's husband had been the quarterback of their high school football team and the nicest boy in school.

"He'll love hearing that. Listen, a couple of us girls from high school want to give you a welcome home tea—" she sent a curious glance at Wynn's bulging tummy "—baby shower sort of thing. I'm sorry I didn't know you were expecting."

"It's okay, Molly. I didn't tell anyone until recently."

Molly glanced over at the women who were openly discussing Wynn at this point. "I understand why. So, can you look at your calendar and give me a couple of Saturday or Sunday afternoons that look clear?"

Wynn blinked. Her high school friends? She didn't know she had any left. "Honestly, my schedule is pretty open. Whatever works for y'all should be fine."

"Okay, then, make us a list of the people you want to invite." Molly reached down and picked up her little girl, who'd run in from the nursery, and settled her on one hip. James followed with the baby.

"It's going to be a pretty small list. I don't have that many friends," she said wryly.

Molly laughed. "I think you'd be surprised at the friends you still have here. Ready, babe?"

"Sure, Mols," James answered. "Good to see you, Wynn." Molly's husband followed Molly out the door, with their baby asleep on his shoulder.

An unexpected pang of envy hit her, and for a second, she wished she'd had someone to be happy with her when she'd found out she was pregnant. Someone walking beside her as she left church, their baby on his shoulder. That wasn't her life, though, and it did no good to wish and wonder about what might have been.

Penny plopped down on the pew beside her, the baby blue gingham dress billowing out around her. She held out a foam cup full of doughnut holes to Wynn. "These are for you, Aunt Wynn. You can fit more in a cup than you can on a plate because you can smash 'em down."

"Good to know. Thanks, Penny."

Joe stuck his head in the door of the church and mouthed, "You got her?"

Wynn nodded. She sat down on the pew beside Penny as the last few people left the sanctuary and took a doughnut hole out of the cup.

Penny sat beside her, her feet up on the pew in front of her. "I know you were scared to come to church, but I'm glad you came anyway." Penny stuck another doughnut hole in her mouth. "I like church."

"I like church, too." Wynn picked up another one of the sticky doughnut pieces and thought about the way her family had stood with her, and how Latham, and Molly, too, had made sure she felt a part of things.

And the church hadn't collapsed when she walked in the doors.

The verse the pastor preached on today, *I'm a new creation*, came back to her. She'd thought when she left Washington, DC, that coming home was going backward when really, it wasn't that at all.

In so many ways, it was a new beginning.

Outside his workshop, Latham lifted the piece he was working on onto a makeshift workbench he'd put together with a couple of sawhorses and a few boards. He'd left Pop inside with Aunt Mae after their Sunday lunch together. The pastor had preached about how through God's mercy, we have a chance to be a new creation every day.

Latham could understand that. When he was working on a piece, the basic bones stayed the same, but as he shaped and sanded, it became new. Every day, there were changes. Each day, a new creation.

He got it. So why did he feel like he was stuck in the past? He had a little sander that he used sometimes for the finishing work, but today, he wanted his muscles to be burning and exhausted so he could just forget everything else.

In church this morning, he'd stood with his arm around Wynn. He wanted her to know that he would stand with her. He'd loved her once, but more, they'd been friends for a long time. Her being pregnant didn't change that.

But what did it change?

Was she still the same person who'd left him on graduation night? Was she a person now who would leave her child with family and go off to chase her own dreams, like his parents left him?

He stopped midstroke with the sandpaper. His own parents had left him because their dreams were stronger than their love for him. He hadn't seen the connection before. Loving Wynn had nearly broken him once. She'd left and he'd had to pick up the pieces of himself.

She'd made a choice, and her choice hadn't been him.

It didn't matter what kind of pretty spin she tried to put on it, the fact was she left. She left *him*.

He pushed the sandpaper down the wood in long even strokes. Was it so much to ask that someone would love him enough to choose to stay?

"Would you like me to leave you alone with your thoughts?" Still in her church clothes, Wynn stood hesitantly at the edge of the woods that lined the clearing around his workshop. "Your aunt told me you were down here."

He picked up a tarp, threw it over his project and walked over to her, taking the bottle of water she held out to him, trying to shake the unfriendly feelings that his thoughts had left him with. "What brings you out here?"

"I didn't get to say goodbye at church. Thanks for sitting with me." Sunglasses covered her eyes, and he couldn't see her expression.

He took a swig of water and motioned to the two Adirondack chairs he had built and placed under a big oak tree. "You're welcome. Although I'm pretty sure Penny had you taken care of."

"She's so precious. Those missing two front teeth are the cutest thing I've ever seen." Wynn sat back in the chair and curled her feet underneath her. "It wasn't as bad as I thought it would be."

"Church? No, it isn't. I mean, there's always a few who have something to say about everything, but most people aren't like that. They really took care of me and Pop after Gran died. I didn't have to cook for at least a couple of months." He picked up a piece of wood from the ground, pulled his pocket-knife out of his pocket and started to slowly peel the layers away, letting the shavings fall at his feet.

"That's really sweet of them. There's a lot I didn't know about this town when I was growing up here."

He shrugged, struggling a little, still, to reconcile the Wynn sitting here with him with the one in his thoughts from a few minutes before. "Why should you? You were a kid— your viewpoint is the only one that matters to you. As you get older, you start to realize there's a lot more to life."

Her eyes were on her hands in her lap. "When you work for the government, you go from crisis to crisis to crisis. And your viewpoint is *always* the only one that matters to you. I know that sounds stupid."

"It doesn't." The birds were twittering in the tree above him, and when he looked up, he could see the clear blue sky through the branches. "It's easy to do. You get caught up in the day-to-day and suddenly realize you haven't looked at the sky in months."

"Okay, maybe not stupid, but selfish. You're so grounded, Latham. I don't see you letting that happen. I don't see you forgetting what's important." Her voice was quiet, and he wondered if it was the sermon that stirred her thoughts.

He shaved small pieces as he turned the wood in his hands, thinking about what she'd said. "When Gran died, I had to reevaluate my life. It was either put Pop in a home and live the life I wanted to lead or live here with

Pop and give up those dreams. I found out it wasn't an either/or decision. I can be the person I wanted to be in Red Hill Springs, just maybe not in the way I imagined it."

She nodded, one hand rubbing her stomach, where he imagined the little one was kicking her. "You know I came home because I needed a safe place to regroup. I didn't plan to stay."

His heart stumbled a second before resuming its normal rhythm, the desire to seize on her words with hope almost overwhelming. He cleared his throat and looked at the piece that was taking shape in his hands. "And now?"

"Like you said, I have to reevaluate. There are some things that are more important than my dreams, and this little girl I'm carrying is one of them. She needs a mom who will put her first and not be calling the babysitter at midnight asking for one more hour because the vote isn't locked in yet."

Tension he didn't even know he'd been carrying eased at her words. She wasn't his mother, putting her needs above those of her child. It wasn't fair to put her in that box.

"Mayor Campbell asked me if I would fill in on the city council until the next election."

He jerked his head up. "What? Charlie finally decided to retire?"

She smiled. "I should've known you'd be dialed in to the local politics."

"I'm not halfway to a PhD in political science for nothin', but his asking you to fill in surprised me." His heart beating like crazy, he asked, "So are you going to do it?"

She hadn't moved from her position in the chair. "I want to. There's a part of me that gets excited about the possibility when I think about it. But I don't want to start something without knowing I'll stay to finish it."

He nodded slowly. "And you're not sure about that now."

"I have to know—really know—that I'm doing the right thing, not just for me, but for her, too."

"I get that. When do you have to give Chip an answer?" He fashioned an eye with the point of his knife.

"Friday."

"That gives you five whole days to make a monumental decision." He raised an eyebrow. "No problem."

"Do you have any advice?"

"Uh-uh, no. This is a decision that you have to make for you and your baby."

Please, please, please, please, please stay.

She nodded once, decisively, and stood, as he put the other eye on the little figure he had carved. "You're right. I have the next five days to figure out what I'm going to do with the rest of my life. Piece of cake, right?"

"Gran told me once that there's nothing ahead that God hasn't already seen, so you don't have to be afraid to make a decision." He walked with her to the edge of the clearing and handed her the little bird he'd made out of the small block of wood. "Just figure out what the most important things are that you want to pass on to your daughter, and that will help you decide."

"Thanks. That helps." She started down the path and turned back, the little carving he made cupped in her hand. "So I'll stay with Pop tomorrow while you take Aunt Mae to the airport?"

"Can you be here around nine? The weather's supposed to get dicey tomorrow afternoon, but I'll be back before then."

"I'll see you in the morning." She gave a little wave and disappeared around the bend.

When she left town the last time, he hadn't had a chance to convince her to change her mind, even though she said he was the only one who could have.

This time, he was choosing to stay silent.

When she stayed—if she did—it would be because *she* wanted to stay, not because he asked her to.

Chapter Twelve

Latham pulled his winter hat farther down on his head and muttered warnings to his truck about going shopping for a shiny new replacement with a heater that worked and leather seats with built-in warmers. The temperature had been dropping like a stone all day, and the heater in his old truck had died about two weeks ago.

He'd dropped Aunt Mae at the airport so she could catch her plane to return to Michigan, where she'd be packing up her house before she moved to Alabama. The icy rain had started as he'd pulled onto the highway. Luckily the season had been fairly mild so far, more like spring weather than winter, but there were winter storm warnings for tonight. In Alabama. He shook his head. In his mind, mild winters and long springs should be the payoff for surviving the hot, humid summers in the South.

Between the road he was on and his house there were two bridges, which he was pretty sure would be iced over since the runways at the airport had been closed two hours ago. The sky was dark gray, the light fading even though it was only afternoon. The boughs on the trees were beginning to bend as the icy rain coated them.

And man, it was cold. He blew his red fingers in an attempt to warm them. The first bridge was just ahead of him. Pulling off onto the shoulder of the road, he grabbed his scarf from the seat beside him, wrapped it around his neck and buttoned up his wool peacoat. After a quick rifle through the dash compartment for gloves and a flashlight, he opened the door and stepped out into the freezing rain.

Cold slammed him in the face, icy water trickling down the back of his neck. He turned the collar up on his coat and started across the bridge. Less than three feet out, he slipped and barely regained his footing. Yeah, the bridge was icy.

It was a little less than a mile to his house from here, and it looked like he was walking it. He picked his way across the bridge and then walked on the shoulder of the road, the grass crunching under his feet. He gauged he was about a quarter of a mile into his walk when a transformer blew with a loud boom and a shower of sparks somewhere between him and his house.

Ice storms like this one were more common in Alabama than snow, and when they came, power outages were inevitable because of the weight of the ice on the trees and power lines. He just hoped that Pop wasn't freaked out by the sudden darkness.

He pulled off one glove and, with fumbling fingers, typed a text to Wynn, who was at his house with Pop. Transformer blew. Y'all okay?

The return text was immediate. We're fine. ETA?

Um. How long did it take to walk three-quarters of a mile in freezing rain? Guessing fifteen minutes.

Be safe.

Fingers shaking, he turned on the flashlight on his phone and then shoved his fingers back into his gloves. Lights on the street this far out into the country were limited to nearby houses and gates. It was dark already, and when the lights went out, it was really dark.

Focusing on putting one foot in front of the other and not slipping, he felt like he was making good time, but he couldn't see the gate to his property through the nasty downpour. He couldn't wait to open the back door of his house and lay eyes on the two most important people in his life.

He didn't mean to think that.

It was the kind of random thought that just meandered through your brain when you weren't paying attention. The kind of random thought that you couldn't escape from once you thought it.

His world looked very different in the dark, covered in ice. He fought a sense of disorientation, and when he finally saw a faint shadow of the drive leading to his home, he breathed a sigh of relief. His ranch-style house sprawled over the hilltop overlooking forty acres. He'd bought the house for practically nothing and restored it himself. It hadn't needed too much. A few walls knocked down to open things up and some TLC, that was all.

Tonight Latham could barely see it, even though he must be getting close. His coat and hat were wet and frozen, his face burning from the cold. The freezing rain was supposed to continue for a few more hours and then, maybe, turn into snow. He didn't know what Wynn's plans were, but no one was going anywhere tonight.

As he got closer to the house, he picked out several spots of a warm yellow-orange glow and realized she'd put a light in every window. Lighting the way home for him.

Yesterday, after church, he'd been frustrated and wondering if she'd ever take a step forward without taking two steps back, and today, she'd literally put a candle in the window for him. He trudged across the yard, his clothes wet and heavy, and finally, he made it to the back door, where he could hear his dogs inside yelping at the door.

Before he could get the door to the mudroom open fully, the dogs were at his side nosing and snuffling his pockets for a snack. He scratched their ears, but he was exhausted and freezing.

A firm tone came from the door that went through to the kitchen. "Teddy, Frank, go lie down."

The German shorthairs cut their eyes at Wynn, but obeyed her command, slinking back into the living room, where he assumed she'd put their bed.

She shut the door behind the dogs and rushed to him. She was beautiful, her pretty hair gleaming in the candlelight. Even wearing leggings and fur-lined boots, she was the prettiest thing he'd ever seen.

"Oh, Latham. You're freezing. Why are you soaking wet?"

"Ha-had to l-leave the truck. B-bridge icy." Now that the exertion of walking through the icy wind and rain had ended, his teeth were chattering, body temp dropping fast. He could barely get the words out and couldn't put thoughts together enough to figure out what to do next.

"Latham. You could've frozen. What if you slid down into a ditch or something?" As she scolded him, she opened the dryer and pulled out towels, setting them on the nearby bench. She unbuttoned his coat and pulled it off as shudders racked him.

"S-sorry. Fingers d-don't work."

"You crazy man, I can't believe you risked your life to get here." His gloves were whisked off next and went with the beanie onto the pile of wet clothes. He didn't even try to answer her, just focused on her voice and how she smelled, inexplicably, of banana bread, as she wrapped a towel around his shoulders and gently rubbed the dampness from his hair.

"Boots." Her voice was firm, but he detected a fine tremor.

"Wynn, no. I can—"

She interrupted him. "Boots. Don't argue. Even if I let you, your fingers wouldn't work."

He sat down on the bench, leaned his head against the wall behind him and set his foot out so she could work at the wet laces.

A few seconds later, he heard his pocket-knife snap open and she sliced through the laces with one quick swipe. "Hey!"

"Hush. Laces are cheap. You need your feet." She sliced through the laces on the other boot. "You take those off now, socks, too, and I'm going to get you some dry clothes. I'll be right back."

Still leaning heavily on the wall behind him, Latham swung his foot over his knee with way more effort than it should've taken and thunked one boot and then the other onto the floor. The mudroom was considerably warmer than outside, but he could still see his breath. He couldn't remember a time when it had been this cold.

Wynn opened the mudroom door and handed him a pair of sweats and a thick pair of wool socks. "The fire's going in the living room. Put these on and I'll have a cup of coffee waiting for you when you're done. Don't dawdle."

She turned around and left the room, closing the door behind her. He stood to do as she instructed and had to laugh. What had she said yesterday? In DC they went from crisis to crisis?

Well, if she handled crises of government with the efficiency she'd just handled him, she must've been pretty good at her job.

Wynn poured the coffee from the carafe she'd filled earlier into an insulated mug. When he'd texted her, she'd had no idea the man had been walking home in the quickly deteriorating weather. He was lucky he was just a little cold. What if he'd fallen and been hurt? He could've died before anyone found him. She stuck a spoon into the sugar, but her hands were shaking so badly, she couldn't get it into the cup. "Stupid, stupid man. He was walking. In this."

"Hey, now." Pop put his arm around her shoulders. "It's all right. He's here and he's fine. A little cold, maybe, but he'll warm up right quick by the fire."

She closed her eyes and turned her face into Pop's flannel shirt. His arms closed around her and he patted her shoulder. "Sweet girl."

The door from the laundry room opened and Latham closed it quickly behind him, tossing his towel on the floor and shoving it in the crack to seal the heat in the room. "Hey, Pop. I heard there was coffee in here."

Wynn handed Latham the mugful of coffee, trying to ignore the pang she got hearing the weariness in his voice. She met his eyes and quickly looked away before he could see all the things she felt that she wasn't ready to even name, much less share. She turned him toward the living room. "Are you hungry?"

"I'm starving. Did you—is it my imagination or do I smell banana bread?" The dogs' tails thumped as he got closer to where they lay by the fire.

Pop laughed as he crossed the room and sat in his recliner, kicking his feet up. "Son, Wynn here has prepared us for snow-mageddon. As soon as we realized we were probably going to get hit by the storm, she started baking. We've got banana bread and brownies. Corn bread to go with the soup that's still warm in the oven. I'm pretty sure there's pumpkin muffins tucked away somewhere in there. She filled every container in the house—including the bathtubs—with water. The thermoses and that carafe are filled with coffee."

"That's really amazing. I can't believe you were able to get all that done." He held his hands out behind him, and she could imagine how good it felt, the fire slowly warming him from the outside as the coffee warmed him from the inside. "Did you let your mom know you're staying here?"

"Yes. I figured the roads wouldn't be passable by the time you got here." She crossed the living room to stand beside him. "We'll have enough wood until morning, probably, and then we'll have to bring in more."

He glanced to the side where he usually kept a small stack of logs, but where she and Pop had stacked as much as they could carry to keep it dry. "Wynn…"

At the warning tone in his voice, she turned to him, eyes wide. "Pop carried the wood. I just helped a little."

He put his arm around her and pulled her into his side. She closed her eyes, just so thankful he was okay. He dropped a kiss in her hair, and the sweetness of that simple gesture loosened the tension coiled inside her.

"You have to be tired. You've been on your feet all day. You sit and I'll bring you supper. Pop? You want some soup?"

Pop waved him off and put his reading glasses on. "I ate some already. I think I'll work on my crossword for a little while, if I can see it."

Wynn shook her head. "No, sir. Your job

is to stay by the fire and recover from that crazy trek through the ice storm."

By the time Wynn came back into the room with their supper, Latham had overtaken one corner of the sofa with a fleece blanket over his legs and Pop was already snoring in his recliner, the crossword book on his chest.

Latham laughed as Wynn handed him a tray. "He'll be like that till morning."

"He worked hard today as my assistant." She settled in the corner of the love seat opposite him and took a spoonful of the soup. She made a face. "It didn't stay as warm as I hoped it would. The oven was still pretty hot when I put it in there."

"It's perfect and so is the corn bread."

"I think you're just hungry because you nearly died." She leveled a stern gaze at him, and he laughed again.

"I'm fine. I wasn't even cold until I stopped moving." He took another bite and then said, "You got an amazing amount accomplished this afternoon."

"It's what I'm good at—breaking a huge task into manageable chunks, making lists, strategizing." She took a bite of the lemon chicken soup. Even if it wasn't piping hot, it was one of her favorites.

"You always were good at that. I remember

you had the homecoming committee hopping the year you were on there."

She tilted her head and shrugged. "I mean, really, all they needed was a little direction, and someone had to be in charge. It turned out great."

"Did you know then that you wanted to be in public service?"

She shot him a grin. "Back then I wanted to be the president. I think I might've been overreaching just a little."

"I wouldn't underestimate that dream. First the city council, then the White House." He smiled, the corner of his mouth tilting up, but she could see a hint of sadness in his eyes.

"I'm beginning to think that a cottage at Red Hill Farm is better than the White House." She surprised herself, saying it out loud, realizing that she was thinking in terms of staying instead of going. She sighed. "You were right when you said that thing about changing the world for Claire and Joe's foster kids. Maybe my perspective is changing, too."

"It happens to the best of us." He rose to his feet. "I'm going for a brownie. Want me to take that for you?"

Wynn handed him her plate. "Do you think you'll ever go back to finish your PhD?"

He put the dishes in the sink of soapy

water that she'd drawn earlier and rubbed the scruffy beard he always had by this time of day. "I don't know. I take a course now and again, when work's not too busy. I get to teach, though, so it's not that much of a compromise when I think about the time I've gotten to spend with Pop."

Staring at the fire, she thought about the years she'd lost with her family when she'd been away. A few holidays weren't the same as living life together. Maybe it was time to return home for good and use what she'd learned to make a better life for the people she loved right here. She couldn't believe she was even thinking it, but as she rubbed the place on her tummy where the baby kicked, there was nothing more perspective-changing than finding yourself unexpectedly pregnant.

Latham came back into the room with a couple of brownies on a paper towel and sprawled out on the floor by the fire. "Join me?"

"For a brownie? Sure." She sat cross-legged opposite him, where she could reach the paper towel. She broke off a piece of the gooey chocolate and popped it in her mouth, elbowing one of the dogs when he got too close to the remainder of her brownie.

She caught Latham's amused glance. "What?"

"If only I'd known in high school that chocolate was the way to your heart." He took a bite and with his mouth full said, "But really, these are unbelievable. What's your secret?"

"If you promise you won't tell..." She laughed as he nodded with another mouthful of brownie. "Cinnamon and chili powder."

He narrowed his eyes at her. "If you don't want to tell me, just say that."

"I'm serious."

"Okay, then. You don't have to worry about my telling anyone. No one would believe it." He rolled to his feet and put another log on the fire, using the poker to get it into just the right position where it burst into flame. "This wood is burning great, but it's so dry, we're going through it like crazy."

"I stacked—I mean, Pop stacked some more right outside the back door under a tarp."

"Mmm-hmm. Pop was so busy today that you need to put your feet up." Latham dropped back to the floor, stretching out his legs beside her. He'd blown out the candles on the last trip to the kitchen. The room was dark, the only light from the flickering flames.

"Oh, I meant to tell you I heard a name the other day that I thought you might like."

"A baby name?"

"Yeah. Have you ever heard of Ada Lovelace?" The light from the fire was mirrored in his eyes.

"I don't think so. Who was she?"

"An Englishwoman who people say was the first computer programmer. In the early eighteen hundreds."

"Wait—*eighteen* hundreds?"

He grinned. "Yes. She was a mathematician and, incidentally, the only legitimate child of Lord Byron. I'd say she had an independent spirit or, at the least, an independent mama since she ended up being about as far from a poet as you can get. So," he shrugged. "Ada."

Wynn stared at him, caught by the simplicity and thoughtfulness of his explanation of a name he'd heard that made him think of her and her baby.

He sat up, abruptly, knee to knee with her. "I'm sorry—did I overstep?"

"No!" She leaned forward, her hands on his knees. "I love it, I absolutely love it. Ada. I was thinking about Jane, too. I loved the book *Jane Eyre*. I loved that Charlotte Bronte made her strong, and even though her life was hard, she never lost the capacity for love."

"Ada Jane. I like it."

Her hand on her tummy, she laughed. "Me, too. It's perfect, actually."

He was so close and just so precious to her, with his strong mind and steady heart. Without thinking, she leaned forward and pressed her lips to his. For a second he hesitated, then gently slid his hand into her hair, his other covering her hand on her belly. He kissed her once, twice, before leaning his forehead against hers.

Insulated against the world and all the decisions and responsibilities, she could only think about him and what he meant to her. *If only. If only.*

She jumped and laughed. "Oh! Did you feel that?"

Taking her hand from underneath his, she pressed it against the spot where she'd felt Ada move. His eyes widened. "Whoa, she's doing flips in there."

Wynn giggled. "She is. I think she likes her name—or the brownies."

His gaze softened. "Wynn—"

"Stop, please. Please don't say anything." She loved his face, the angles and curves highlighted now by the fire, and her fingers itched for her sketchbook. His deep brown eyes were on hers, the laughter gone, replaced by a wariness she wished that she hadn't put there. "Just for tonight, can we let this be what it is and not talk about it?"

He looked into her eyes for a moment longer and brushed a kiss across her lips. "Okay. We won't talk about it tonight."

Pushing to his feet, he said, "I'm going to bring in more wood so we have enough to last till morning. Need anything?"

"No, I'm good." She watched him go, then crawled onto the couch, curling up in the corner, her arms wrapped around baby Ada, the warmth and glow of the fire soothing her into a lull of contentment.

She barely registered the cold air when the door opened and he brought the firewood in, but through her almost closed eyes, she saw him tuck a blanket around Pop in his recliner. A few seconds later, she felt him tuck one around her, too.

He settled at the end of the couch, his hand on her feet. She could see only his silhouette as he watched the fire, but he was standing guard so she could sleep, safe and warm.

Chapter Thirteen

"Thanks for the hospitality." Wynn turned to Latham, her eyes bright blue against the white, white world, a police SUV her brother had sent for her idling in the drive. The dogs were romping in the yard, but his eyes were only for her.

"I'll be snowed in with you anytime." Latham smiled, but he wasn't ready to say goodbye, didn't want that cocoon they'd been in last night to be invaded by anyone.

He unwound the scarf from his neck and wrapped it around hers, just like he had in the church courtyard. "Stay warm."

Her heart in her eyes, she said, "Latham…"

"Hey, we're not talking about it, remember?" The look in her eyes worried him. She'd been subdued all morning, and he couldn't stop thinking that maybe the kisses that had felt so right last night were exactly the wrong thing to do, pushing her into "retreat" mode.

"All right, then. I'll see you around." She backed away. "It was fun."

He whistled for the dogs and laughed as they tore across the unfamiliar white stuff. When he looked up, the SUV was halfway down the drive. He followed the dogs into the house and poured a lukewarm cup of coffee from one of the carafes Wynn had filled yesterday. He crossed slowly to the plateglass picture window, and watched as the SUV turned onto the highway.

"Feels a little less warm in here without Wynn brightening the place up." Pop stopped beside Latham at the window, buttoning up his favorite burgundy cardigan.

"Yeah, it does." Latham turned away from the window. "I guess I'll stoke up the fire. The officer Joe sent out for Wynn said it might be another day before we get our power back."

His grandfather stepped in his way. "Are you going to let her go without a fight?"

"I don't know what you mean." Latham had a feeling that he knew exactly what Pop meant, but he really didn't want to talk about it. Why was it so wrong for him to want her to choose him, fight for him?

"Anyone with eyes can see you have feelings for Wynn. Are you in love with her or not?" Pop's bushy gray eyebrows came together in a V as he scowled at Latham.

Latham sighed. Pop saw too much, but that wasn't a surprise. He lifted his hands, palms up, misery like a hard rock in his belly. "I think I've been in love with her since we were in junior high school."

Pop nodded slowly, like a kindergarten teacher to a slow pupil. "Then give her a reason to stay. Give her a hundred reasons."

Latham paced away, but in the small kitchen, there was nowhere to run. "If I do that, and she stays, I don't want her to resent me for being the one to cap her dreams."

Pop made a dismissive noise. "You kids and your dreams, like everybody always gets to do what they want. Do you think it was my big dream to be a shopkeeper? All my life I've loved to tinker with things. If I could've gone to college, I would've studied engineering. My father owned the store before me, and after he passed away, we found dozens of nature journals full of drawings of plants and birds and streams. Do you think he was unhappy? Do you think I was?" Pop's voice broke. "My years with Margenia were the best years of my life. All fifty-nine of them.

Some things are more important than following your own dreams."

Latham realized that Pop had just spoken about Gran in past tense, something he hadn't done, not even once, since Gran died. "Pop? Let's sit down."

"I don't want to sit down. I've been sitting," Pop snapped.

Treading carefully, Latham said, "You know Gran is gone."

His grandfather's watery eyes filled with tears that he was too stubborn to let fall. "Yes. She was killed in a car accident."

"I'm so sorry, Pop."

"I know you are, bud." Pop stared out the window at the bright blue sky, unblinking, and for a second, Latham thought he'd lost him. But then Pop said, "At first it was just random pockets of time where I'd remember she was gone. And then, more and more. The kids pull you into the future, you know? Not for you, for them."

"I know." Latham thought his heart might actually break in two. He loved this man so much—owed this man so much.

Pop put a gnarled hand on the windowsill. That hand had taught Latham to fish and whittle and had smoothed his hair when he was sick more times than Latham could count. "I think somewhere inside I knew it." He paused again. "I like the kids at the farm. I think Margenia would be proud of how I'm teaching them to do math."

Latham's throat closed up, but he choked out the words. "I think so, too. I think she would be really proud."

"She would be proud of you, too." Pop's face was grooved with grief, but also with joy. His lips trembled as he smiled at Latham, but his eyes that had been clouded with confusion were clear. "Listen, here's what I've learned in these past seventy-eight years. Sometimes there's a difference between our dreams and God's plans. Maybe it's how He teaches us that His ways are better, I don't know. But what I do know is that Wynn won't resent you if you're in this life together. You'll boost each other up. Simple as that."

Latham nodded slowly. "Maybe you're right."

Pop clapped his hands and rubbed his palms together. "Now, where's that big diamond I gave your grandmother on our fiftieth wedding anniversary?"

"In the safe-deposit box."

Pop shuffled back to his recliner in his old slippers, sat down and popped up the footrest. "You get that ring and put it in your pocket.

Think about what it would mean to live life with Wynn, because that's what marriage is. It's not about you get your dream and I don't get mine, or you give up your dream while I get what I want. It's about building new dreams together." He shook open yesterday's paper and began reading it.

"Pop…"

"Hush, boy. Can't you see I'm about to take a nap?"

Latham opened his mouth and closed it again, eyes stinging with tears. Would this clarity of mind for Pop last? Maybe. He didn't know, but he was so grateful for these moments, when he could understand the wisdom of lessons Pop had learned from a lifetime of living and loving.

Wynn sat in the corner of the sofa in her newly renovated space, the air still smelling of paint and spackle and freshly sawed wood. She stared at the fire, the crackle and hiss of the wood the only sound in her quiet cottage.

Joe and Claire had invited her to stay at the main house until the power came back on. They'd had a generator installed after a particularly bad storm when they were dating, but their house was full of kids and family, loud and boisterous, and overwhelming.

Sometimes that was just what she needed, but right now, she needed some peace to think.

The words she'd thought last night were repeating themselves in her brain over and over again. *If only. If only. If only.*

If only, what? If only she hadn't gone to Washington, DC, and been stupid enough to fall for her narcissistic boss? If only she hadn't left on graduation night?

If only she'd realized that the boy she loved in high school was the one she'd love for the rest of her life?

Yeah, that one was a punch in the gut.

Because it was too late—if she asked Latham for another chance, she would be asking him to take on another life change he hadn't planned on, and the forever commitment of instant fatherhood. She shook her head. No, he deserved his space to be the person he wanted to be, had planned to be, every bit as much as she did.

She heard the squeals and feet hitting her porch just before the door slammed open, and her laughing sisters-in-law spilled into the room. Both were dressed in sweatpants and boots, with a variety of hats and scarves, and she was pretty sure that Jordan was wearing gardening gloves. Claire was clutching a gallon of rocky road and three spoons.

Wynn quickly shut the door behind them, and when she turned, they were already at the fireplace, shedding layers. "What is this?"

"Claire and I decided it was time to initiate you into a secret sisterly tradition."

Claire raised one eyebrow at her twin. "Is it really secret?"

"Shh. She has to understand how solemn an occasion this is." Jordan stopped and stared at Wynn. "Seriously, how do you do that?"

"What?" Wynn looked at Claire, who shrugged.

"Look like you just stepped out of a catalog shoot. Claire and I look like we've been through the Peloponnesian Wars. I think Sparta won again."

"Ice cream, Jordan." Claire eased down to the floor in front of the fire.

"Right. So, when Claire and I are having a hard time, we break out the rocky road. It's a little-known fact that ice cream has the power to soothe the soul and loosen the lips."

Claire laughed. "You weren't supposed to tell her that part."

"Oh, right. Forget the part about loosening lips." Jordan grinned as she pulled the top off the ice cream. "Truthfully, Claire and I just had to get out of the madhouse up there. After two days of being cooped in the house, the kids aren't the only ones going crazy."

"I think this is a sisterly tradition I can get behind." Wynn sat on the floor next to Jordan, grabbed a spoon and took a bite of the ice cream. "Rocky road is my favorite."

Claire dug her spoon into the container. "So, you got stranded at Latham's house."

Wynn looked from one curious face to the other. "Yes. Nothing happened. We were all in the living room the whole time—me and Latham and his seventy-eight-year-old grandpa."

Jordan licked ice cream off her spoon. "Come on, give us the real scoop. The chemistry between the two of you is so obvious. You have a past—that much we already know. But is there a future for the two of you?"

Wynn had held that future in her hand once. The futility of hoping for another chance with all that stood between them was overwhelming. She burst into tears.

"Now look what you did, Jordan." Claire took another bite of ice cream, the mother of many unfazed by Wynn's tears.

Wynn mopped at her face. "It's not Jordan's fault. It's mine. I'm such a mess."

"It can't be that bad. Let's talk it through."

Jordan stuck her spoon into the container of ice cream and let it sit.

"There's just so much up in the air about my life right now. And I never do anything without a plan."

Claire nodded. "I get that. I'm the same way. So, start with the basics. You have a place to live here for as long as you want it. Do you want to stay in Red Hill Springs for the long term?"

Wynn hadn't admitted it, not even to herself, but she did want to stay. She'd loved being in Washington, DC, the power center, but she'd been untethered there somehow. Here she felt grounded. She could remember who she was.

She nodded slowly. "I love it here, but I have to be able to support myself and the baby. I have to have a job—a real job."

"Okay, we'll be praying about that." Claire picked up her spoon and took another bite of ice cream. "What about Latham? You guys do have a long history together. Do you have feelings for him?"

Tears filled her eyes again. She nodded. "But six months ago, I was convinced I was in love with my boss, until I saw his engagement announcement in the paper—to another woman."

"What? That jerk!" Jordan frowned. "No wonder you came home a little gun-shy."

Wynn sighed. "Yeah, there's that, and the fact that I'm six and a half months pregnant."

The three of them heaved a simultaneous sigh.

Claire's calm voice broke through to Wynn. "Is what you feel for Latham different from what you felt for your boss?"

"Yes. Definitely." She jabbed her fingers through her hair. "I tried to forget him when I left home. I had myself convinced I'd forgotten him a long time ago. But he's just so…"

"Handsome," Jordan said. "He's really handsome."

Claire nodded. "Steady, too."

"He is. He's smart and gorgeous and steady. The total package. I just don't know if I'm drawn to that because my life is so unstable right now, or if I really have been in love with him since I was fourteen, because the truth is, that's what it feels like." She lifted a hand and let it drop, the waterworks starting again.

Tears sprang into Claire's eyes, too. "That guy you were dating is a real jerk, Wynn, but I think you can trust Latham."

"I trust him, it's not that. I just don't trust myself. I've always been so sure of myself, and now—I have to do something and I just feel paralyzed. I don't know what to do."

Jordan capped the ice cream and set her spoon on top of the carton. "You're smart enough to know you have to tell him how you feel."

Her eyes sprang open. "I thought of that, but I can't. It's really not fair to him."

"Here's the beauty—you don't get to decide what's fair to him, he does. Tell him."

"Would you feel better if you made a plan and then you tell him?" Claire's orderly thinking once again cut through Wynn's panicked thoughts.

"Yes, having a plan would help. Okay, so I make a plan, then I tell him?"

Claire patted her knee. "Yes, exactly. You can do it when you've got everything in order."

"Right. I feel better," Wynn said, but her chest still felt tight. She had housing and that was a piece of the puzzle, but there were custody issues to be settled and she needed a job. She felt like then she would be at a place where she could talk to Latham on equal footing. And that was important to her.

"It's the ice cream," Jordan said, hauling Claire gently to her feet.

"No." Wynn shook her head and grabbed

her sisters-in-law, now friends, in for a hug. "It's you guys."

They loaded all the layers back on. Claire dug a flashlight out of her pocket and turned to Wynn. "Come up to the house if you get cold or lonely. Chances are I'll be awake no matter what time."

"Thanks. You guys are the best." She hugged them again, thanking God that her brothers had the good sense to choose them.

After they left, Wynn picked up her laptop, which whirred to life when she opened it. She had some plans to make, and when she was done, she would decide what to do about Latham. She cared about him—there was no denying that now, but the thought of actually saying it out loud made her want to run away.

She'd tried running away once. She wasn't doing it again. This time, she was going to try her best to make her life here. Details were still sketchy, but when she got it sorted out, she would tell Latham how she felt, and what happened from there would be up to him.

It took two more days for the roads to thaw out enough for life to get back to normal in south Alabama and another couple of days before Latham could make it to the bank. But he found himself standing in the vault with the safe-deposit box in front of him on the table, sifting through a lifetime of odds and ends that Pop had entrusted the bank with.

A brown and crumbly envelope held his and Gran's Social Security cards. A wedding picture of Latham's two grandparents from 1959. A will that Pop kept trying to get Latham to read. On top were several jewelry cases. One held the pearls that Gran's mother had given her on her sixteenth birthday. One held her wedding rings, the ones she'd worn their whole marriage. The other held the one Pop got her for their fiftieth wedding anniversary with five stones, one for each decade they'd been married.

Latham remembered the party, but Pop had given Gran the ring when they were alone. He'd caught them dancing in the kitchen, Gran hiding her hand under her apron before she laughed and held it out for Latham to admire. He'd pretended to be blinded by the light.

He chuckled to himself now, at the memory. He had so many like that, so many examples of what life together should be. He could imagine that beautiful ring on Wynn's finger and her dancing in the kitchen they shared.

Maybe he shouldn't push her. Maybe he shouldn't ask at all. He didn't know her plans.

He wasn't even sure *she* knew her plans at this point, but if she went back to Washington, DC, or any of the other places around the world that she could find a job, he would never forgive himself if he hadn't told her how he felt.

So this time, he would ask. And this time, if she was leaving, she would have to say goodbye.

He stuck the ring box in his jeans pocket and closed the lid on the safe-deposit box with a sense of determination. He strolled back through the bank and waved at the manager. "See you later, Henry."

Henry stuck his head out of the glassed-in office. "You better be recruiting hard for your church league softball team. I picked up a ringer last week."

"Oh, yeah?" Latham grinned. "Our team came in first last year and we didn't even practice. Just think what we can do if we get some time in the batting cage."

"Book the time. You're gonna need it."

Latham was still laughing at Henry's boasts when he opened the door of the bank. He could tell from the unbelievably tempting aroma of baked goods that Jules was back in her kitchen at Take the Cake. He started across the street to pick up a sack of doughnut holes for Pop when he noted a black Suburban he'd never seen before at the Hilltop Café.

It wasn't unusual to see people passing through from other places—Bertie's food was the best around—but something about this one made the hair on the back of his neck stand on end.

Just as he got to the curb, the front door to the Hilltop swung open and a man came out. Recognition slammed Latham. He knew the slick city haircut and tailored suit from pictures he'd seen of Congressman Schofield, Wynn's former boss.

He had a bad feeling about this. From what he knew, and that wasn't much, Wynn and Schofield hadn't parted on good terms. And he wondered if Schofield was here to get back his girlfriend, or his right-hand assistant.

Either way, it couldn't be good.

Chapter Fourteen

Wynn had forgotten how much she loved to paint, pouring out her feelings on paper. When she was a teenager, she'd play the most emotional songs she could find and paint for hours.

For years, she'd pushed that part of herself away, focusing on the analytical and concrete. Thinking back now, she wondered if she would've been an even better strategist if she'd acknowledged the feelings pulsing underneath Washington's superficial surface. Probably not. Because feelings didn't matter. The vote did.

She swayed a little as music filled her studio. She loved the way the paper felt under the brush, how the paint spread in a loose flow of color. She even loved how she had just a moment to influence the paint on the page before it set. She could paint over it, but that color, that layer, remained.

Kind of like life. The present was a layer of color that could still be manipulated and changed. The past was set. It could be painted over, but it would always be a part of the painting. If the artist was skillful, though, even the past layers gave a beautiful, complicated depth to the finished product.

Stepping back, she looked at the painting from a distance before adding a little more color. Drama was fine in a painting, but in her life she could've done with a little less depth and a little more tranquility, to be honest.

Hearing something, she picked up the remote for her speaker and muted the music.

Definitely a knock at the door. It wouldn't be one of the kids at this hour. Maybe Claire and the baby?

She ran down the stairs in her bare feet, brushes still in hand, and pulled open the door with a smile.

When she saw Preston standing on her doorstep, the smile faded. She tried to look at him with cold detachment, but her heart was slamming in her chest. She'd be a stuck pig before she'd let him see it. "What are you doing here, Preston?"

He straightened the sleeves on his pristine

suit coat and adjusted the cuffs, something she'd thought was an adorable quirk when she was dating him. Now she recognized it was a nervous habit. "Aren't you going to invite me in, Wynn?"

When she turned to pull the door open farther, she caught the sound of his indrawn breath as he saw her stomach from the side. She closed the door, and when she turned around, his face was red. "I thought we agreed that having a child together wasn't a good idea."

She walked to the kitchen sink and turned the water on, taking her time to rinse her brushes one by one. "*We're* not doing anything together. A baby isn't something you can legislate away, Preston. It's a baby."

He shrugged. "You have no proof it's even mine."

That statement was so ridiculous Wynn didn't even bother to reply.

Preston walked closer to the granite island standing between him and where she was standing at the sink. "You made the decision to keep it, so that's on you. I'm not imploding my career because you didn't have the guts to do what needed to be done."

"Wow, you really are a piece of work, aren't you?"

"That's what I've been told." He grinned,

a powerful, feral smile that she'd once found tantalizing. Now she recognized it as an attempt to exert his control over her.

"What are you doing here, Preston? How did you even know where to find me?"

He leaned an elbow on the counter, noticed a little construction dust and straightened, brushing invisible dirt off his sleeve. "Your mother told me. I think she likes me."

"Trust me, she doesn't."

Walking into the living room, he slid his left hand, the one with the gleaming gold watch on the wrist, into one pants pocket. She was blown away as she realized how much of what he did was for effect.

He turned back, an earnest look in his eyes. "I think you left DC because you were angry, and I get that. But I want to give you a chance to think it over. If you want to come back, we can make it happen."

"I don't think so. Anything else?"

He held his hands out, palms up. "Wynn, I know the engagement announcement threw you, but you have to understand that's all politics. We can still keep seeing each other in private, if that's what you want."

She stared at him, the absolute gall of what he was saying leaving her speechless.

Deliberately, she dried her hands and

folded the kitchen towel into precise fourths before walking into the living area. "I'm not coming back. Not for any reason, and definitely not to have an affair with you."

She saw the facade crack just a little, but he said, "I don't need you."

The desire to throw him out of her house and out of her life was so strong. But she had more than herself to think about. She gestured at the blue velvet sofa. "Would you like to sit? I don't have coffee, but I can fix you an herbal tea."

He glanced at her sharply as he sat. "No. Thanks."

She sat in the chair at a ninety-degree angle to the sofa, avoiding cradling her belly, even though she felt a desperate need to protect Ada Jane. "I'm having a baby, Preston."

"I can see that," he snapped.

"I'm willing to stay away from national politics completely." She waited a minute for him to catch up.

He raised one eyebrow. "Oh, I get it. This is a negotiation. I should've known."

"Yes, you should have." She folded her hands in her lap.

"It will never have my name and I will never acknowledge it as a Schofield."

"All right."

"I'm serious, Wynn. If you try to get a penny out of me or my family, I will destroy you." The expression on his face didn't change as he threatened her, and that was perhaps the scariest thing of all about him. His political aspirations eclipsed anything in his life, even a person he'd claimed to care about. Even his own child.

She rose, and as confidently as she could in bare feet, walked to the desk, removing a sheaf of papers in a plain manila envelope, thanking God that Claire encouraged her to have a plan. When she put them on the coffee table in front of him, she said, "These papers release you from any and all parental rights. They stipulate that you relinquish those rights willingly and without coercion of any kind."

He held out his hand, and she laid a pen in his palm. "We could put all this behind us and go back to the way things were. I know you miss me," he said.

She didn't. She really, really didn't. And that was the thing that allowed her to be calm in the face of his narcissistic onslaught. "Sign the papers, Preston. This all goes away—me, the baby, the potential harm to your political aspirations."

Preston glanced over the paperwork, and like he had the entire time she'd worked for him, trusted that what she said was true. He scrawled his name across the bottom of the page. What he didn't realize was that by signing away his rights, he was acknowledging the paternity of the child. The assertion wouldn't hold up in court, but it would likely be enough to request DNA testing if Ada Jane ever desired it.

Wynn took the signed papers and returned them to her desk drawer. "It's time for you to go."

He stood, straightening his suit coat and buttoning the top button before he walked to the door, shaking his head. "I think you're making a big mistake, Wynn. You could've been somebody in Washington."

So many things ran through her mind right then that she could've said in retort, but nothing she said would change his opinion, and he'd only cemented her opinion of him. So instead, she held the door open for him and watched him pick his way around the path back to the driveway, trying not to get his expensive shoes muddy.

It was a little humiliating that she'd been so taken in by him, to the point that she'd lost herself. She walked over to the desk, pulled out the papers she'd prepared and looked at the scrawled signature. He'd just given her the best gift he could possibly give her—the chance to raise her daughter free of his influence. There would be questions and there would be a time to answer them, but that would be on Ada Jane's terms.

She drew in a breath and blew it out, a long stream of pent-up anxiety gone. Now it was time to move on.

Latham dipped his paintbrush into the paint and cut around the edge of one wall with pale blue paint. His hands were busy here, but his mind was with Wynn, wondering what happened when her former boss found her.

"So I want to know who decided we would paint instead of play soccer," Ash grumbled as he unscrewed the blinds from the window casing.

Joe was following behind Latham with the roller. "It's too cold for soccer."

"So we're painting instead?" Ash scowled.

"No, Joe and I are painting. *You're* complaining," Latham said, then felt guilty for snapping at Ash. It wasn't his fault that his sister's ex was in town, or that Latham had a diamond ring burning a hole in his pocket. "Sorry."

"What are you fixing this room up for?" Joe pushed the roller into the tray of paint.

"Aunt Mae is moving here to live with me and Pop. I talked to her last night. She said to tell the kids she misses them." Latham dripped blue paint onto the glossy white trim and growled.

Ash, on a stepladder at the window, swiveled his head to look at Latham. "What is wrong with you? You've been in a horrible mood ever since…"

Latham didn't turn around.

"Ever since Wynn got back into town." Joe finished the sentence for him.

Latham ignored him, too.

Ash stepped down and sat on the top step of the ladder. "I don't blame you for being annoyed. She had you renovating that whole house."

Joe grinned at his brother while he loaded more paint onto the roller. "And she's always at his house. I bet she bosses him around. She loved to boss us around when we were kids."

"She probably eats a lot, too," Ash said.

"That's all you can think of? She eats a lot?" Latham asked, without turning around.

"Okay, that was a stretch. But something's got you stirred up. What's going on?"

"Nothing. It's just that congressman being in town today. He looks like a fancy, phony jerk. I don't know what she saw in him."

Latham kept his eyes on the line he was painting, but inside he was stirred up and he didn't like the feeling.

Joe put the roller slowly down in the tray and leaned on it. "What congressman?"

His voice was low and deadly, more cop than friend, and Latham looked up, surprised. "The one she used to work for. I've seen his picture, and he was at the Hilltop this morning."

"I'll kill him if he hurt her." Ash's mouth was a firm, flat line. "Or, you know, have a serious talk with him."

Latham winced slightly. He'd stirred up the brotherly wrath of the Sheehan boys, but it would serve that idiot right if they descended on him like ugly on an ape.

"He was all slick, like Ash when he gets all dressed up." Latham kept painting, the simple motion somehow holding him together.

"Hey!" Ash looked incensed. "Seriously, I'm right here."

"Did he talk to Mom?" Joe's arms were crossed.

Latham shrugged, a jerky frustrated movement. "I guess. He came out of the Hilltop."

"What do you think he wants?" Ash scooted the stepladder to the other window and picked up the screwdriver.

"Maybe he wants her to come back to work for him. He's engaged to someone else, right?" Joe was still glowering.

"Surely he's not dumb enough to think he can get her back." Ash contributed this from the window.

"You don't think she'll want to go back to DC?" Latham sat back on his heels and tossed the brush he was using onto the plastic. He wished he could be as certain as Ash. He wanted to believe she wouldn't leave, but she'd said herself when she first came home that she had no idea how long she would stay.

He'd thought things had shifted the night of the storm, but with Wynn, who knew?

"Of course she's not gonna go with him." Ash dropped the blinds onto the bed in the center of the room.

"I'm going to talk to her." Joe looked around. "Do you want me to wrap that roller before I go?"

"I'm going, too." Ash laid the screwdriver onto the dresser. "Latham?"

"No." He wanted to go, wanted to look her in the eyes and see how she was, see if she'd been hurt again by that guy. See if her feelings for him had changed. But it wasn't his place.

If she wanted to talk to him about it, she knew where to find him.

* * *

Wynn had stayed to herself in the cottage all afternoon. Penny came by after school and had a chocolate chip cookie with her in front of the fire, but didn't stay long.

Regaining the peace she'd felt before Preston invaded her space had been impossible, but she wasn't upset, just a little sad. She wasn't even sure why, except that she hadn't heard from Latham at all. She'd thought for sure after the snow and ice melted that he would show up to make sure her roof hadn't leaked, at least, but her phone had been silent.

A soft knock at the door sounded, and her heartbeat picked up. Maybe she'd been worried for nothing. But when she pulled the door open, it was her mom. Bertie had a take-out sack in one hand and a cake carrier balanced on the other one.

Wynn's lip trembled, and for a second she wasn't sure if she was going to smile or cry. "Chocolate cake?"

"And a cheeseburger, double bacon and Cajun fries. Mickey made it special for you. I figured you wouldn't feel much like getting out today."

"You figured right." She took the cake from her mom, put it on the bar and got a drink out of the fridge, meeting her mom at the coffee table.

She pulled the cheeseburger out of the bag and rolled back the paper so she could take a bite. Her mom put the fries on a napkin, helping herself to a few.

Wynn hadn't realized how hungry she was. She hadn't really had food in the house, so she'd just nibbled on some popcorn and an apple and cheese. Now that she'd had the first bite of the familiar comfort food, she was suddenly ravenous. She polished off the cheeseburger in about two seconds and licked the ketchup off her fingers.

Her mom handed her a napkin, and she wiped her mouth. "That was perfect, thanks."

"Would you like to talk about today?"

"You mean about what happened with Preston? Yeah, thanks for telling him where I live now."

"I figured you needed some closure." Bertie picked up a fry and bit the end off.

"Well, I got closure, all right." Wynn stuffed the wrapper down in the bag. "I think it's safe to say that he won't be back."

"What did he want?"

Wynn rolled her eyes. "He actually thought I'd want to go back to DC with him and pick up where we left off."

Someone pounded on her door. She sent her mom a concerned look, but then her brother Ash shouted through the door. "Come on, Wynn, open up."

"What in the world?" She awkwardly got to her feet—her growing belly making it a little hard to do anything gracefully these days—walked to the door and pulled it open.

Both of her brothers were standing on the front porch, their arms crossed. She stepped out of the doorway and gestured into the room. "Boys—"

Ash came in first and gave a low whistle. "This place looks great. I love the loft."

"Thanks. Me, too."

"Wow, it actually looks kind of classy now." Joe crossed the living room and kissed their mom. "What are you doing here?"

Bertie shoved the fries toward him. "The same thing you are, most likely."

"Is this chocolate cake?" Ash tapped the cake carrier.

"Yes," Wynn said. "It's mine, but I'll share if you'll get out of my kitchen." She pushed him away, but he didn't go far, waiting until she sliced four big pieces of cake onto her pale blue dessert plates before helping her carry them into the living room.

Joe started the inquisition. "So where were you in the story when we came in?"

"I was just getting started."

"Okay, start over." Joe sat back, making his cake disappear at an alarming rate.

"The short version is that he thought I would come back to DC and pick up where we left off. I disagreed."

Ash smiled. "I said that's what you would do."

Her mother was being quiet, and no one in their family was ever quiet. "Mom?"

"What did he say about the baby?"

Wynn sighed. "He was surprised that I was actually pregnant. He doesn't want anything to do with a baby, or any strings attached to that baby. And since he was so clear about it, I had him sign papers relinquishing his parental rights."

"Oh, honey." Her mom's eyes were on hers, and for once, her brothers were silent.

Tears puddled in her eyes, but she refused to let them fall. "There's no reason to pretend that he would ever want to be involved. This way, I don't have to worry about him showing up someday and trying to get custody of her."

"Brilliant." Joe stuffed the last bite of cake into his mouth. "I'm proud of you, sis."

"Me, too," Ash said. He sat down on the

couch next to her and knuckle-rubbed her head. "He's a real jerk and you deserve better."

"I know. But thanks for saying it."

Joe looked at his watch. "I've got to get home. I'll be back for another piece of cake tomorrow."

She grinned as he kissed her on the head. "Okay, if there's any left by then, you've got dibs."

"I'm going, too. I'll talk to you tomorrow." Ash followed Joe out the door, the two of them much more subdued than when they arrived.

Her mom laid her fork down on the plate. "Latham was outside the diner today when Preston was there. He didn't say anything to me, but I'm pretty sure he recognized him. He's got to be wondering what happened."

Latham saw Preston? Her stomach sank. "I'll talk to him tomorrow. He deserves to hear about it from me."

"Wynn, I don't know what's going on with you and Latham now, or really even what happened in the past. I do know if you love him, you shouldn't deprive him of that love because *you* think you might not be right for him."

"My life's not simple right now." And it

wasn't. But she was making plans to stay, wasn't she?

Her mother smiled. "Nor will it ever be, darling."

Wynn collected the plates and walked her mom to the door. "Thanks for coming tonight. It was good not to be alone."

Watching her mom go, she thought about the conversation she would have with Latham tomorrow. He must have been stunned to see Preston in Red Hill Springs, every bit as much as she was. Preston had no hold on her anymore. She just hoped Latham would believe it.

Chapter Fifteen

Saturday morning, the day after Preston's surprise visit to Red Hill Springs, Pop went to breakfast with the Old Geezers Club, as they called themselves, and Latham set out to replenish their wood supply, which was drastically diminished after the ice storm.

He swung the ax and split the wood. Maybe the physical exercise would exorcise some of the fears haunting his dreams last night. He hadn't slept well and, consequently, was in a foul mood this morning. He kept telling himself he shouldn't be worried about the congressman's visit, but the truth was, Preston Schofield had a claim on Wynn and a history with her that Latham didn't have. That ate at him, along with the fact that he'd let Pop talk him into getting the ring out of the safe-deposit box and carrying it in his pocket where he couldn't forget about it.

Ever.

A car stopped in the driveway as he sent the last two pieces of the log flying off the chopping block. He stuck the cutting edge of the ax into one of the pieces and walked over to meet Wynn in the driveway. "Hey, did your mom drop you off to pick up your car?"

Her eyes were shadowed, the skin underneath looking fragile, and he wondered if she'd stayed awake all night last night like he did. She blinked at him in the bright sun. "I thought maybe we could have a cup of coffee, if you have time."

"I have time. Pop's out to breakfast with his friends." He held open the door for her to enter and closed it behind them. "Do you want something to eat? There's some banana bread left, I think."

"No, thanks."

He reached into the cabinet for a couple of mugs and poured coffee from the carafe, sliding hers over for her to doctor.

"My brothers told me you saw Preston in town yesterday." She stirred sugar into her coffee and followed it with cream.

Latham picked up his mug, trying to figure out how to ask diplomatically. Finally, he just said what he was thinking. "What was he doing here?"

She opened her mouth to answer, and he put his hand up. "No, wait. I shouldn't be asking you that." He waved a hand in the general direction of her stomach. "He has every reason to be here, and it's none of my business."

A fact that galled him.

"C'mon, let's go sit on the porch." She didn't wait for him to answer, just walked through the back door and settled in a rocker, looking out over his land, the coffee mug cradled in her slim fingers.

When he sat down beside her, she said, "I can tell you're not happy with me. I want you to tell me why."

"I'm not unhappy with you, but seeing him stirred me up inside." All this time, he'd slowly been convincing himself that she could feel the same way about him that he felt about her.

"I don't really understand. Unless you thought I might go back to him."

"Would you?" He paced to the edge of the deck, setting his coffee cup on the railing, looking out over the fields, but not really seeing them.

"No! Preston asked me to come back to

Washington and work with him. I turned him down."

He swung around to face her. "What did he say about the baby?"

She took in a shaky breath. "Well, he doesn't want anything from his past to hinder his political aspirations."

"He's a first-class jerk."

"Precisely." She walked to the rail and stood beside him. "What's bothering you, Latham?"

She'd been honest with him. Spilling his guts wasn't exactly something he relished, but he could return the favor. "I guess seeing him just brought home the fact that you could leave anytime. There's nothing really holding you here."

"That's not true. I have my family. I have a home here." Her hand touched his, and he wanted to grasp hold.

"I know, but your goals have always been for something bigger, brighter, more important maybe, than what you could find in Red Hill Springs." And she'd made him no promises. She hadn't really even told him how she felt about him. They'd shared some kisses, which made him think there was something there, but it wouldn't be the first time he'd been wrong about Wynn. How could he trust her—when everything had changed and nothing had changed?

She looked at him with those clear blue eyes. "You're right. I did want those things—and I was confused about what was really important. I'm starting to figure that out now."

He stuck his hand in his pocket, his fingers finding the diamond ring. "You've told me yourself you don't know what the future holds for you here."

Tension laced her voice. "I *don't* know, but I'm working on it. I just need you to give me a little time to make some plans."

He'd been thinking of asking her to marry him. Since he'd picked up that ring yesterday, and before, if he was honest with himself, he'd been imagining life with her. He just wasn't sure she was doing the same. "Look. You haven't made any commitment to me. I get that. It just slapped me in the face when I saw the congressman, that if you got a job somewhere, you'd leave."

"For now, I'm staying." She spread her hands. "That's all I've got, but I'm trying."

Now wasn't enough. Maybe that wasn't fair to her. Maybe it wasn't even fair to himself, but he couldn't do this. He couldn't put his heart in her hands again. "Look, I'm just a country boy with half a PhD. I can't compete with the Preston Schofields of the world."

"They can't hold a candle to you."

He wanted to believe that she meant it, that he had a chance with her. That one day, when they were old and gray, they'd be dancing in the kitchen together. He just wasn't sure he could. "I guess I need some time, too."

"Okay. You can have as much time as you need." Her phone buzzed, and she dug in her purse to find it. She checked the screen and then said, "I have to go. I'll see you around."

He watched her leave. He wanted to chase her car down the drive and beg her not to go. He was in love with her.

He couldn't do that, though. She had to stay because she wanted to, not because he needed her to.

When she was out of sight of Latham's house, Wynn pulled over to the side of the road and let her tears fall. It had been just an awful two days.

She'd been ready for the showdown with Preston, although she definitely hadn't expected the grief that came along with her daughter's biological father wanting to write her out of his life for the sake of convenience. Ada Jane would be better off without him.

But Latham… Wynn had thought he'd want to know what happened with Preston, but she hadn't expected that the surprise visit would make Latham question *her*. She let out a long wavering sigh.

Maybe that was for the best, too. If he was still questioning her loyalty because of what she'd done ten years ago, she couldn't blame him. It hurt her feelings a little, but he needed to work through it.

She swiped the tears from her face and put the car in gear. It was kind of ironic that she was trying to get her life together so she could go to him on equal footing and tell him she was in love with him.

His uncertainty made her question her whole decision to tell him how she felt. Maybe she was trying too hard to make things fit. She'd done that with Preston, and that hadn't exactly turned out well.

Her mom had texted and asked her to come straight to the church. Maybe it would get her mind off all the things she couldn't control to help her mom with her latest project, and then she would stop for one of Jules's chocolate cupcakes on her way home.

Wynn pulled into the parking lot and groaned when she saw it loaded with cars. What had her mother dragged her into? She looked in the rearview mirror, wiped the mascara from under her eyes and fluffed her hair.

A few scattered raindrops were falling from the sky, and she ran for the door of the fellowship hall, flinging it open and skidding to a stop when she saw the room was filled with pink balloons and streamers. Her friends—many of whom she hadn't seen since high school—were standing around in groups. She recognized her mother's friends, too, and all the repair work she'd done on her mascara was for naught.

"Surprise!" Jordan grabbed her by the elbow and dragged her into the room. "Molly figured you would never give her a list, so we decided to surprise you!"

As people realized she'd arrived, they started to gather around her, offering congratulations.

"Y'all. I can't even believe this. Thank you so much!" She smiled at the familiar faces and got a laugh when she waved at the food table stacked high with tiny pink cupcakes, little cocktail-sized sandwiches and fancy decorated cookies. "Please, eat and talk… and eat. Look at all that food!"

The true joy of people she'd known her whole life, but hadn't seen in years, proved to her that she was in the right place. She was surrounded by people who had her back no matter what she'd done. Here in Red Hill Springs, she was finding everything she needed—except the faith of the one person she needed to believe in her most.

To find the organizers of this ambush, she went straight to the kitchen. Molly was pulling a tray of sausage balls out of the oven and Jules was putting tiny cheesecakes on a tray. "I *will* get you back for this one day when you least expect it."

Jules whirled around, a guilty flush creeping up her cheeks. "Wynn! Molly, I told you we were going to be on borrowed time."

Molly smiled and tossed the sausage balls into a basket lined with a pink napkin. "I'm willing to take that chance. I'm really happy you're back in town, and I want you to stay."

Was there never an end to the tears that she would shed during this pregnancy? "Thank you. I'm trying to make a plan for the future. Just not sure of all the details yet."

"Good. Let's go into the fellowship hall. It's time to get the games started."

Wynn gripped the edge of the kitchen counter, images of silliness with straw and cotton balls and stickers on her forehead filling her head. "Games?"

Molly laughed and tucked her arm through

Wynn's. "Just kidding. I said I want you to stay, not go running for the first flight out of here."

Following Molly through the fellowship hall, Wynn greeted half a dozen friends from high school, her algebra teacher, two of her mother's best friends and Lanna from the diner. She was seated in a chair at one end of the circle, her face muscles straining from the effort of looking like she was happy and having a good time.

Jordan handed her a plate and sat down next to her. She had a notebook on her lap. "You okay? You look a little tense."

"I'm fine. What's the notebook for?"

Her sister-in-law had on an actual dress and boots today, her red hair in a loose waterfall down her back. "I'm writing down the gifts that you get so you don't have to try to remember who to write thank-you notes to."

"That's a good idea."

"Have you never been to one of these things before?"

Wynn shrugged her shoulders. "I don't think so. I worked seven days a week. I remember being invited to a few between college and law school, but I did a summer start program for law school so I could graduate early."

"Of course you did."

"I was ambitious, and see where it got me? Jobless in Red Hill Springs." She took a bite of a sausage ball as Jordan laughed at her. "Wow, this is really good."

"Hey, Jordan." Mary Pat Haney, whose married last name completely escaped Wynn, slid into the seat next to her and gave her a shy hug. "I heard you were home. I'm sorry I haven't been by to see you."

Mary Pat was a curvy blonde, and if she was still the same as when they were kids, one of the sweetest people Wynn had ever met. "No worries. Life has been kind of chaotic for everyone. What are you doing back in Red Hill Springs?"

A deep breath from Mary Pat alerted Wynn to the fact that she might've just stuck her foot in her mouth. "You know what, if you don't want to talk about your life, I'm your girl."

Mary Pat laughed, her cheeks pink. "Thanks. It's not a big deal and I should be over the embarrassment by now. I have two boys and I got a divorce about a year ago and moved home to be with my dad."

So Wynn wasn't the only one who'd come home to recover from life. What did you say to someone who just told you about her divorce? Ignoring it seemed like a sound policy. "I bet the boys love the farm."

"They do. They're covered in mud all the time and happy as they can be. My dad is—well, he's just the best."

"Are you working? I'm sure keeping up with the boys is a full-time job."

"It definitely could be, but I finished nursing school after I moved here and got a job in Mobile." Mary Pat ate a tiny cucumber sandwich. "What about you? Do you have any plans?"

"That's the million-dollar question these days. I don't. Not yet." Maybe if she had, she wouldn't be avoiding thinking about Latham because those tears were too close to the surface.

"That has to be hard on you, especially with a baby coming." Mary Pat's eyes were understanding, and for once, Wynn didn't feel defensive.

"It is hard. When I first got home, I needed some time to think and recover—honestly—from a bad relationship. Now I'm ready to have a plan and I have some feelers out, but no job offers yet."

"I understand completely. It looks like Jules

is ready for you to open presents, but call me and let's get lunch some time."

"I'd love that," Wynn said, surprised that she meant it. For months now, she'd wanted to hide from the residents of Red Hill Springs, and the rest of the world. Maybe that she was ready now was a sign.

Mary Pat slipped out of the chair, and Jules piled packages on it. She handed Wynn one wrapped in white paper with little pink footprints. "From Lanna."

Her chest started to hurt.

She tore off the paper and pulled the box open. It was a tiny footed sleeper with dancing bears on it and a book called *Wherever You Are*. She held it up and all the ladies gave a collective sigh. "Thanks, Lanna. I love it."

"I read that book to my grandkids. It's a tearjerker."

Awesome. Wynn definitely needed a board book that would make her cry when she read it.

"Pass it around," Jules said.

"What?"

"Pass the gift around. People want to see them up close." Jules handed her another package as Wynn handed that one to Jordan.

"You really have never been to a shower before. You're socially inept."

"I'm not. Put me in the middle of a political fundraiser and I'm the life of the party."

Her sister sighed. "Just open the present. This one is from Claire."

Claire's gift was a basket of baby-proofing items. She looked up and met her sister-in-law's eyes with a smile. "Thank you!"

"It happens so fast. One day they stay where you put them, the next day they've crawled to an outlet and tried to stick their finger in it. I'm speaking hypothetically, of course." Claire grinned, the new baby asleep in her arms.

Wynn tried to imagine taking her baby with her places, and she just came up with a blank. It was so foreign to her.

A vibrating bouncy seat, a basket of toiletries for the baby, tiny socks, tiny T-shirts, tiny baby gowns. Her sister and mom had gone in together for a car seat system. Wynn didn't even know there was such a thing, but it was amazing.

The ladies who had thrown the shower gave her a video baby monitor, which she was sure she would never need because the baby was going to be in her sight at all times.

When it was over, she cried again as she told them all thank you. "I feel very loved. This is the most amazing 'welcome home—baby shower' anyone has ever had. Thank you all for coming."

She stood by the door and hugged and thanked each one again personally, and by the time they all left, she was dead on her feet. Her mom put her arm around her. "We packed up the leftovers for you and put them in your car. The gifts have been loaded and they're on their way to be delivered to the cottage. Are you okay?"

Wynn hugged her mom. "Yes. This was so nice. I don't deserve how nice everyone has been to me."

"Oh, sweet girl. Of course you do. Now go home, fix yourself a plate because I know you didn't get to eat, and put your feet up."

She drove home in a fog of exhaustion, and when she got home, she was shocked to see Latham's truck parked in the driveway. Her heart raced as she tried to think with her tired mind what she would say to him.

She opened the door and picked up the boxes of leftovers her mom had packed up. She met Latham walking around the path from the cottage.

"I put the gifts in the room you're using as a nursery. I hope that's okay."

So, they weren't going to exchange pleasantries, then. "Thank you. You didn't have to do that."

"Your mom asked me to since I have the truck."

So he wanted her to know he hadn't come for her, but as a favor to her mom. The tears were back, in her throat, behind her eyes, but she didn't give in to them. She'd cried enough today. "Well, I appreciate it. I guess I'll see you later."

He nodded, but he didn't smile, and she wondered if she had done that to him, if she had taken away his easy smile. She walked the rest of the way around the pond, almost desperate to get inside. So much had happened today that she couldn't even process it.

A light was on in the nursery, and Latham had stacked the gifts just inside the door. The baby room didn't have furniture yet, and it seemed so empty.

Across the pond, she heard Latham's truck start with a growl. He was upset with her, and still he'd brought the gifts over because her mom had asked him to. She wished things were different and that he could be sitting here with her, looking through the gifts for Ada Jane.

She flipped the light off and walked back into the living area, sitting on the couch and swinging her feet up. Her belly tightened in a Braxton Hicks contraction. She'd been having more lately. Her doctor told her it was just the body's way of practicing to have a baby.

Ready or not, the baby was coming soon. And Ada Jane deserved a mom who had a plan.

Chapter Sixteen

"Wynn Sheehan?"

Wynn stopped short on the street outside the Hilltop and slowly turned around. A man she'd never seen before, around thirty-five, in khaki pants and a button-down with the sleeves rolled up, gave her a little wave from the door of his office.

"Can I help you?"

He smiled and his face creased into friendly dimples. "Your mom told me I might catch you. Come in for a bad cup of coffee?"

She was on her way to the obstetrician for a checkup, but she had a few minutes. "Okay… sure. I'll just have water, though."

"Wise choice. I make terrible coffee." The man pushed the door to his office open wider, and she thought for a second that this seemed too much like a TV movie and she should probably run for her life, but she'd been seeing his office for months now and wondering about it, so she followed him inside.

He gestured to a group of two leather seats. He had nice eyes that crinkled when he smiled and riotous brown hair that was completely unprofessional. "I'm Garrett Cole. I'm an attorney. Your mom said you're a lawyer, too. Or she said you went to law school. Sorry, I'm not that clear on the details."

He spoke as he walked to the back of the long room, where there was a counter with a sink. He grabbed a paper cup and filled it with water from the tap.

"I'm licensed in Alabama," Wynn said, "but I haven't practiced. I worked on Congressman Schofield's staff up until a few months ago."

He handed her the cup of water. "I heard that. I also heard you were good at it. Do you have any interest in being a part of a firm?" Garrett grinned.

"If you're talking about your firm, I might. I'd like to stay in Red Hill Springs. I don't know anything at all about this kind of practice." She was intrigued, though.

"It's kind of a learn-on-the-job deal. The short answer is I do a little bit of everything. I have too much work to do on my own, plus I'm going to have to be away soon for a month, so I need a partner, or at least someone to help with my cases for a while."

"You don't even know me. How do you know I'd make a good partner?"

"I don't." He shrugged. "But I've met you now. I like you. And Chip Campbell vouched for you. He said he asked you to be on the town council. I like that you'll be involved in the community and that you have family ties here."

"Chip told you that?" She took a sip of the water and looked around. The building had one wall of exposed brick and the ceiling was open. There was the grouping of two leather chairs and one desk a little farther back closer to the counter where he kept the coffeepot, but there was plenty of space for her to have a desk and for an assistant if there was one. This office was two doors down from Jules's bakery and three down from the Hilltop. She'd be working in very close proximity to her family.

She considered for a second if that would bother her and decided it wouldn't. "So you told me the short answer of what you do. How about the long one?"

"I handle estate planning, the occasional criminal case, family law, bankruptcy, even a personal injury case or two." He hung his hand over the arm of his chair, and a black-and-white cat with a curious pink nose came out to rub her head against his hand. "Here's the thing. It sounds silly, but I became an attorney so I could help people. People come to me when they don't have any other options, and I help them. It's mostly really fulfilling, sometimes frustrating, but it's always interesting."

He paused. "Oh, and the cat comes with the office."

"I like cats." Her mind was racing through the possibilities, shuffling through her feelings. This had the potential to be everything she'd been looking for. "So how would this work?"

"If you want to start work before your baby comes, I can give you a case or two to handle now. And then while I'm away, you'll take care of my cases. When I get back, if you like the work, we can talk about your buying into the practice. If not, I'll say thanks for the help and no hard feelings."

"You'll put all that in writing." After all, they were attorneys. They didn't trust a handshake.

His grin was wide. "Of course. So you're interested?"

"I am. Very interested."

"Any more questions or requests?"

She thought for a second. "I'm planning to breastfeed. I'll either have my baby with me or be pumping."

His color went pink. "Of course. That's totally fine. One of the benefits of working solo in a small town is that I make the rules."

"I've been praying for an opportunity to stay close to Red Hill Springs. I really appreciate the offer." Wynn was having trouble believing that her prayer had been answered in a way that filled all of her needs.

"You're an answer to a specific prayer for me, too." Garrett leaned forward and held out his hand. "Looking forward to getting to know you better."

"Me, too." She rose and he stood, as well. "I guess I'd better go let Chip know that I'm available for the town council."

"I guess I'd better start shopping for another desk." He held the door open for her. "I'll get the paperwork drawn up and give you a call and we can make it official."

"Thank you." She walked out the door of the law office and turned back. The nameplate on the door said Garrett Cole, Attorney at Law. She hoped this worked out. Maybe there would be another name added to the door before long.

She checked her watch and started down the street to her car, her feet feeling ten thousand pounds lighter than they had a few hours ago. Maybe after her OB appointment, she would go see Latham at work. She had a job, and that felt like the last piece of the puzzle falling into place.

It wasn't permanent—yet—but she had a good feeling.

Latham sat at a table in the courtyard outside his classroom with a plate of tacos from the food truck that parked outside his building, skimming over his notes for the day. He looked up as someone slid a plate onto the table opposite him, expecting one of his students.

Instead, Wynn sat across from him, a plate of nachos piled high with beans and guacamole in front of her. She stuffed one in her mouth and said, "Wow, if I'd known there was such good food on campus, I'd have come a long time ago."

"You should check out the doughnut truck some time." His eyes were on hers. He had no idea what she was doing there. It wasn't like they'd parted on the best of terms, and he wasn't ready to move forward unless things had changed.

"You're probably wondering what I'm doing here." She echoed his thoughts as she popped another nacho into her mouth. "Aside from getting this extremely tasty late lunch, that is."

"The thought crossed my mind." His heart literally ached looking at her. She was dressed casually in jeans and boots, a T-shirt and a long necklace with a tassel hanging off it. Her hair was long and loose, and her blue eyes were covered with tortoise shell sunglasses.

She rubbed her belly absentmindedly. "I know you probably already have a lesson planned, but if you want me to talk to your freshman class and answer questions, I'd be happy to. Today, or another time, if you'd rather."

"I'm not sure what your motivation is, here."

"I feel like I'm on firmer ground now than I was when you first asked me. I wondered then if I could say anything helpful, and I'm still not sure I could've. Now I feel like I can contribute. And you asked me to."

The words slugged him. He shrugged and tried to make it nonchalant, like it didn't really matter that she was there. But it did. It really did matter that she'd taken the time to come down there because he asked her to. "Okay."

"Okay, you want me to talk?" Her face lit up. "Awesome."

"Just don't say anything embarrassing."

She grinned. "I promise. No stories from our misspent youth."

He stood, picked up his plate and hers, too, walking over to the trash can and dumping them. She could always get to him, a fact that didn't exactly make him comfortable. "All right, let's go. You can talk as long as you want and then we'll do questions for the rest of the time. Suit you?"

"Yes."

The class was mostly waiting for him when they walked in the door. There would inevitably be a few stragglers. He took the strap for his case from over his shoulder and placed the bag on the desk, sat on the edge and waited for the class to quiet. "Okay, guys, we have a special guest this afternoon. This is Wynn Sheehan. She was a staffer in Washington, DC, for the last four years. She's got the inside scoop on what life is like inside the Beltway and might even be able to give you some hints about how to get a job. Wynn, the floor's yours."

He walked to the back of the room and

watched as she effortlessly reeled them in. She talked about how every decision she made as a student had an effect on her job—which was something these students needed to hear.

It served him right, he guessed, that he was as attracted to her brain as to her beauty. She was the whole package. If he knew she would stay… Gran's diamond ring was a hard knot in his pocket, reminding him what was at stake.

He wanted her to come to him and make promises. Maybe her coming here today was her version of a peace offering, he didn't know. What he did know is that she held his heart, in no uncertain terms.

He dragged his attention back to her words. "So, in Washington, DC, I was on Congressman Schofield's staff. My official title was Legislative Director. I had a small staff of people under me who all had expertise in a variety of policy areas. Each of those people was responsible for keeping up with legislation and major issues that might be coming up in their area of expertise and advising me and the chief of staff, especially if it would affect the people in the district we were serving. Got it so far?"

Someone in the middle of the room raised

her hand. "So if there's a bill that your congressperson is trying to get passed, who writes that?"

"It could be someone like me, or sometimes a junior staffer is assigned a bill to write. They check in with the Office of Legislative Counsel and are assigned a lawyer who helps turn the bill into legislative-speak. Often these are run by advocacy groups, too, before they're presented to the member of Congress. Then he or she will sign the bill and it goes into the hopper."

Another hand went up. "And then does the bill come before the House for a vote?"

"Sometimes. More often, those small bills end up bundled in with larger pieces of legislation." Wynn leaned on the desk, her hand rubbing the side of her baby belly. Latham wondered if the baby was kicking her.

"Is it exciting to work there?" This from a young woman Latham knew had aspirations to go to law school.

Wynn smiled. "It really is. I guess maybe some people get jaded to the whole process, but I never did. It was exciting to be at the center of lawmaking in our country, to know that the things that we worked on that eventually became law had the power to change things for people. Real people who lived real lives, not just statistics."

One of the students in the back of the room closed his book. Latham glanced at his watch, shocked that an hour had gone by. He stood. "That's it for today, guys. Let's thank our guest."

There was some scattered applause as the students gathered their books and left. Wynn grabbed the young lady who'd asked the question about working in DC being exciting and handed her a card. Leave it to Wynn to narrow in on the one student with real interest.

When the room was empty except for the two of them, he leaned on the desk beside her. "Thanks for coming. You managed to intrigue and inspire a class of college students…and their teacher."

Her hand rubbed circles on her tummy. "It was my pleasure. I'm sorry I wouldn't come before. I had a hard time accepting that my life had changed so much, especially because it was my fault. I guess now I'm starting to realize that God is big enough to use even my mistakes." She shrugged a little. "It's a process."

He walked outside with her and lingered on the sidewalk. "I'm sorry—I know I've put pressure on you. And you're right, it's not easy. It took me some time after Gran died to come to grips with the fact that not only had I lost one person I loved, but the other one was barely hanging on."

She took a couple of steps toward her car and swayed a little, then turned around. "Do you want to come over for dessert? I have a couple of boxes of goodies left from the shower."

"I don't know, Wynn." This visit had been great, but ultimately, nothing had changed. Seeing her in action this evening just made him realize even more that she was meant for bigger things. She was made for it.

"Just to talk. I want to tell you about—" She grabbed her belly with a low groan. "Oh. Wow."

He gripped her elbow. "Are you okay?"

She looked up at him, a look of panic in her eyes, and he watched as all the color drained from her face. Her eyes drifted away from his and she swayed again, going limp in his arms.

"Wynn!"

He sank to the ground with her and dug his phone out of his satchel, dialing 911 with shaking fingers. "I'm just outside the Sanger building at the junior college. A pregnant woman passed out."

With the phone clutched in his hand and

the promise from the dispatcher that EMTs would be on their way, he shook her gently. "Wynn, wake up. Come on, love, wake up."

She roused slightly, opening groggy blue eyes. Her lips moved, like she was trying to make words, but nothing came out and she was gone again.

"Where is that ambulance? *Come on.*" He stared unblinking into her pale, pale face and prayed.

Please God, please. You've brought her back to me. Please, God, let her be okay. Let Ada be okay. Oh, God, why is this happening?

The paramedics took seven long minutes to arrive and about thirty seconds to get her on a gurney. They loaded her into the ambulance, where one guy started working on her. Latham thought he saw her eyes open, but he wasn't sure.

The other EMT stood in front of him. "Hey, sir, we're gonna take good care of her, but I need you to talk to me for a second. Tell me what happened."

"We were just walking. She asked me if I wanted to go get some dessert and then she grabbed her stomach. She—um—she went white and her eyes rolled back in her head. I grabbed her as she fell." He could barely get the words out, and his gaze went to Wynn in the back of the ambulance.

"How many weeks pregnant is she?" The EMT snapped out the question.

"Around seven months—twenty-eight weeks—I think." Latham didn't look at him. The guy in the ambulance had an IV hanging.

"'Scuse me, sir. Just a couple more questions. How long has she been bleeding?"

He looked at the EMT, then. "She wasn't bleeding."

The one in the back of the ambulance snapped his fingers at the guy talking to Latham. "Sam. Let's go."

The EMT—Sam—said, "You can meet us at Mercy," then jumped into the driver's seat. The big engine growled, and seconds later, lights and sirens went on.

When he looked down, Latham realized his pants, where Wynn had been lying across his lap, were covered in blood. "I didn't know."

He stood in the parking lot staring at her purse on the ground. A couple of students came out of the building.

One of them stopped, looking concerned, but keeping his distance. "Hey, dude. You okay?"

The words jolted him into action. He picked up Wynn's purse, ran to his truck and jumped inside. With trembling fingers, he scrolled through his contacts until he found Wynn's mom. *Come on, come on.*

She didn't answer.

He dialed Joe, closing his eyes when Joe answered.

"Joe, it's Latham. Wynn's in an ambulance on the way to the hospital in Mobile."

"Which one?"

"Mercy." Latham started the truck and backed out of the parking space.

"I'll get everybody there. What happened?"

"She passed out. She was bleeding, Joe." Latham pulled out into the street, wincing as a car blew past him, honking the horn.

"Pay attention to the drive, Latham. She's gonna be okay. The baby's gonna be fine, too. We'll meet you there."

Latham wanted to believe Joe, but all he could think was how stupid and careless he had been. The woman he loved had been in his arms and he was too scared to tell her he loved her. And he loved Ada Jane already.

Lord, please let her be okay.

She had to be okay, and then he would tell her. He would tell her over and over until she believed him.

He wasn't making that mistake again.

Chapter Seventeen

Wynn reached up to scratch her face. Her fingers found an oxygen mask. She opened her eyes.

She was in a bed with a rough white sheet. There were cabinets, a door. Her eyes drifted closed, her head aching. The last thing she remembered, she'd been at the college, walking outside with Latham. Snatches of memory drifted up…an ambulance…sirens.

Her eyes snapped open and her hands searched out her tummy, where Ada grew, and tears slid down the side of her face as she realized the baby was still there. Ada Jane moved under her hands, and she breathed, *Thank you, Jesus.*

Her belly was wrapped in two wide elastic bands. She looked around to see if she could figure out what they were hooked to and saw the tiny heart blipping on the monitor. *Thank you, Jesus, thank you.*

The door opened and Latham came in, dressed in scrubs. He was at her side in a second. "Hey, you."

"Hey." Her voice sounded raspy, muffled by the plastic on her face. She looked up at him, and the sweet concern in his eyes undid her. She pulled the oxygen mask off as the tears started again. "What happened?"

"I'm not sure. One minute you were talking, the next you were falling." His voice shook, and she reached for his hand.

"You called the ambulance?"

"Yes." He looked down at their hands, tracing the lines of her palm with his thumb.

"Ada Jane's okay?"

He met her eyes. "Her heartbeat's strong. I think they're going to do an ultrasound, too." He looked away for a second, and she knew there was something else. He took a deep breath. "There was some bleeding—a lot of bleeding—and they have to figure out what was causing it."

"Okay." There were feelings spinning in her head that she couldn't even bring together as coherent thoughts. She was responsible for this little life growing inside her, and she could've lost her. How did you put that into words?

"Your family's on their way. They might be here now, if you want me to get them."

She tightened her grip on his hand. "No, not yet. Will you stay with me until we know?"

He brushed her hair away from her face with a tender and gentle hand. "I'll be right here as long as you want me."

Forever. She wanted him forever. The thought popped into her head, but in her heart, she knew it was true.

The door opened, and Mary Pat Haney came in, dressed in light blue scrubs, and pushing a portable machine. "Hey, you're awake. Good. We're going to do an ultrasound and see what's going on with your little one."

"Any idea what happened?"

"The ambulance brought you in. According to the EMT, you lost a good bit of blood and passed out." Mary Pat checked the flow on the IV. "We're giving you some fluids now, which should help."

"How lucky did I have to be to get you as my nurse?"

Mary Pat grinned as she checked the strip scrolling out of the fetal monitor. "Not that lucky. I work in the ER here four days a week."

"Am I having contractions?"

Mary Pat held out the strip and pointed to a couple of small waves. "Yes, here and here. Those are contractions, but not the kind that lead to premature delivery. We'll keep an eye on them and make sure, but most likely, these are due to the general irritability of the area."

"I'm so out of my league here. I haven't even started childbirth classes yet."

Her nurse laughed and pulled Wynn's shirt up over her tummy. "I think you'll have plenty of time. Do you need some privacy, or are we good?"

Wynn's eyes darted to Latham's and back to Mary Pat. "We're good."

"Okay, then. Ready to see this little girl?"

"Yes." Wynn was suddenly scared again. Her palms went sweaty, her eyes glued to the monitor.

Latham squeezed her hand. "I bet she's grown since the last time we saw her."

Mary Pat typed in a few things, then squirted the gel on and started sliding the wand around on Wynn's stomach. She lifted the wand and tried again. "Ah, there's Baby Girl's heart. It looks perfect."

Wynn wanted to be strong, but the sound of that heartbeat filling the room made her cry again. It was so beautiful and steady.

Mary Pat squinted at the screen, moving

the wand, holding it, tap-tapping the keys, taking measurements. "The amount of fluid around the baby looks good." She ran the wand around the side of Wynn's belly. "Okay. Let's see if we can get a look at her face, just so you can rest easy."

She ran the wand across Wynn's upper abdomen and around. "There she is."

The image wasn't as clear as with the ultrasound at the doctor's office, but Wynn could see the little eyes and nose and mouth.

Latham's eyes were on the monitor, too. "Thank God."

His voice was shaking with emotion, and Mary Pat glanced over at him with a curious look. She didn't ask, though, just took the wand off of Wynn's belly, wiped the gel away and handed her a tissue.

Her old friend backed out the door with the portable ultrasound. "You rest, Wynn. The doctor will be in to talk to you in a few minutes."

Before the door had closed completely, it opened again and Bertie rushed in, concern for her own child on her face. "The people at the desk said I could come back. Are you okay, baby?"

Wynn burst into tears, and the worried look on Bertie's face softened. She took Wynn's other hand. "You and my granddaughter are going to be just fine."

Bertie looked at Latham over Wynn's head, the question in her eyes. He nodded. "She's going to be okay."

A soft knock sounded at the door just before it was pushed open by a doctor in scrubs and a white coat.

"I'm Dr. Dearling." He shook hands with Bertie and Latham and patted Wynn on the leg before checking the strip on the monitor. He looked at it for a couple of seconds and then stepped to the side where he could see Wynn's face. "So, here's where we are. The baby's looking good. Your vital signs are good. I looked at the ultrasound film. The ultrasound showed that your placenta is low in the uterus—a condition called placenta previa. The bleeding was probably caused by your exam at the doctor today."

"Will the condition affect the baby?"

"No. She'll continue growing just like she has been. The hope is that the condition will resolve itself. If it doesn't, you'll be scheduled for a C-section a few days before your due date."

It wasn't the way she'd imagined it going, but if she could deliver a healthy baby, she didn't care.

The doctor pulled the computer monitor close to him and started typing while he talked. "We want you to rest and stay off your feet for the next couple of days and then take it easy for the rest of your pregnancy. No heavy lifting or strenuous exercise. Got it?"

"I'm going home?"

He glanced up from the computer monitor where he'd been typing and smiled. "Yes, we're cutting you loose. Once you sign the discharge papers, you'll be good to go."

"I'll take you home and stay with you tonight," Bertie said, her tone leaving no room for argument.

Wynn looked at Latham. There were things that she wanted to say—needed to say. If nothing else, today had shown her that life wasn't a given.

She didn't want to wait any longer.

As if she suddenly realized the tension in the room, Bertie said, "I'm gonna run out and share what's going on with Jules and Joe. I'll be right back, Wynn."

With Bertie gone, Latham sat on the edge of the bed, facing Wynn. He hadn't let go of her hand since he first came in. "I don't want to take my eyes off of you. That twenty minutes or so between the time the ambulance took you and the time I saw you again was the longest twenty minutes of my life."

"I love you, Latham." The words came easily to her now, and she wondered why she'd waited so long to just tell him how she felt.

His eyes went glossy and he looked away, and for a second she froze. But his gaze came back to hers, and his face was so full of love that she could barely breathe.

He smiled down at her. "Do you remember when we were in eighth grade, and I fell out of Ash's tree house and broke my arm?"

She nodded.

"You wouldn't leave my side until Gran got there, and you threatened to punch Ash in the face because he laughed when I cried a little. I fell in love with you that day. I haven't stopped loving you since." He brushed his fingers down her cheek, sliding them around to cup her neck as he leaned forward to kiss her, like it was the most natural thing in the world.

His lips hovered over hers, and she held his face with both of her hands, just breathing.

The door opened, and her mother came in, took in the scene and backed out into the hall again.

Latham smiled into Wynn's eyes and kissed her. "Can I come see you tomorrow?"

"Yes, if you bring doughnuts."

He laughed as he opened the door. "I wouldn't dare show up without doughnuts."

The next morning, Latham picked up their favorite twists at Take the Cake and got to Red Hill Farm around nine. He knew it was early. Wynn might even still be asleep. He just couldn't wait to see her.

He picked up the bag of doughnuts, walked around the pond and knocked on the door to Wynn's cottage.

Bertie answered, her purse over her shoulder. "Hey, Latham. I was just heading over to the Hilltop. You'll be able to stick around today?"

"I plan on sticking around a lot longer than just today."

Wynn's mom laughed. "Well, then. I wish you luck."

Wynn appeared in the door as Bertie was leaving. She looked a little tired, a smudge of purple under her beautiful blue eyes, but she had color in her face again. "Hey, I thought I heard you out here."

"You're not supposed to be on your feet."

"Well, I had to answer the door." She took the bag from his hands and opened it. "Oh, these smell so good."

"Want to sit on the porch swing? It's quiet out here. Kids are in school."

"Sure." She grabbed a long sweater from the chair beside the door and wrapped it around her, settling in the swing beside him, putting her feet on the wooden crate he nudged over in front of her.

He offered her a doughnut, and they swung and ate for a minute. The morning was peaceful. The pond was still, the surface shiny, the grass beginning to green up as the weather warmed. Birds chattered in the trees, and a soft breeze whispered through the pine trees. He realized with Wynn beside him, he was content. "I didn't sleep much last night. I kept replaying all that happened and just praying, thanking God that you and Ada are okay."

"I know. I slept but every time I woke up, I kept remembering waking up in the hospital and not knowing how I got there."

He swung them for a few beats. "I love you, Wynn. I know I said it last night, but I want you to hear me say it in the light of day. I love you. No qualifications, no reservations. I just…love you."

Wynn sniffed, and he handed her a napkin out of the doughnut bag to wipe her eyes. "I got a job. It's here in Red Hill Springs."

"Where?"

"I'm going to be working with Garrett Cole in his law practice. It's different from anything I've ever done, but I'm having a baby. My life would be different anyway."

His heart was so full. She'd made a choice and she was staying. "That's great, Wynn. Congratulations."

"I told Mayor Campbell that I'd take Charlie's position on the town council, too. It doesn't pay anything except a small token honorarium, but I want to contribute." She turned to him. "This is silly, but I've always thought of myself as having wings. Red Hill Springs might be a home base, but I'd fly off to other places to live my life. I know now that Red Hill Springs is also where my roots are, and those roots are deep. I want my daughter to be grounded here."

She paused. "I didn't know I could love a person as much as I love you. I fought so hard against it. It didn't seem right or fair to bring my crazy, messed-up life into yours. But the more I tried to fight it, the more I realized that you've always been it for me. All the years in between disappeared as soon as I saw you again. I'm not leaving."

That was all he needed to hear.

He dug in his pocket with trembling fingers and pulled out the ring his grandpa had given him. "You don't have to promise me that. If you decided to leave, I'd figure out a way to go with you. If it's all or nothing, I choose all. Please marry me, Wynn."

She was openly crying now, but she held out her hand for him to slide the ring onto her finger. "It's the most beautiful thing I've ever seen."

His leather satchel was next to the swing on the porch floor. He reached into it and pulled out a box and handed it to her. "This is for you, too."

She pulled the top off and breathed a slow, "Oh!"

He'd fashioned a bird's nest and had carved three smooth, shiny eggs out of mahogany. Attached to the nest was a brown kraft paper tag. She pulled it out and read the words on it out loud, "*I am no bird; and no net ensnares me; I am a free human being with an independent will.*" She turned, searching out his eyes. "*Jane Eyre?*"

"You said you liked the book. I've been reading it." He took a deep, shaky breath. He wasn't sure he was going to say this well, even now. "The nest is home. The three eggs—those are you and me and Ada—our family."

Her lip trembled. "And the quote?"

"The next part of the quote, the part I didn't write there, says, *which I now exert to leave you*. You've always had a vision beyond yourself, Wynn. That certainty about your calling is what drew me to you all those years ago. I don't want you to change that part of you. Our home is here because you choose it, not because I would force you to stay. It's important to me that you know that."

She grabbed his face between her two hands and kissed him—a warm, solid, tear-salty kiss. "I love you. *You* make dreams come true that I didn't even know I had. I can't wait to see the adventures we'll have together."

His hand slid around her tummy, cradling it in his big palm. "Our Ada Jane is going to be very loved."

"And so are you." Wynn smiled and kissed him.

With Wynn in his arms to stay, Latham knew that the years of waiting in between their first kiss and the first kiss of their new life together had been worth it.

Epilogue

Once again, Latham stood beside a hospital bed wearing scrubs...and the most adorable expression of abject love Wynn had ever seen, as he looked down at Ada Jane's tiny red face.

Wynn smiled up at her husband and brand-new baby girl. "Less than an hour old, and she's already got you wrapped around her itty-bitty finger."

"She does, and that's absolutely as it should be. Baby girl, you had Daddy's heart from the first second I saw you." He kissed Ada's forehead and gently lowered her into Wynn's arms. "Just like your mama. Oh, honey, you did so good."

The door opened. Claire and Joe came in with a giant bouquet of pink balloons. Penny skipped beside them, but when she saw Latham, she ran to him, giggling as he lifted her into his arms and tossed her in the air.

"A certain someone insisted that her baby sister would like balloons better than flowers." Joe tied them to the edge of the rolling tray beside the bed and grinned down at his sister and new baby niece. "She's pretty cute. You did good, sis."

"You want to see her?" Latham asked Penny, who nodded her head vigorously, blond ponytails bobbing. When Penny became free for adoption a few weeks after Wynn and Latham got married, they'd moved quickly to add the sweet little girl to their family. A week later, a judge had given them custody, and they'd be finalizing the adoption next month.

She might not have been born to them, but Penny was their daughter in every way that counted, and she was thriving as permanency became more of a reality. And she wasn't the only one—Pop doted on her, now that he truly was *her* grandpa.

Latham set Penny down on the bed beside Wynn, who snuggled the little girl into her side and eased the baby over so Penny could see.

"She's so sweet," Penny said, as she touched

Ada's hand with one fingertip, the nail painted pale pink.

Latham kissed Wynn on the head. "I'm the luckiest man in the world to have my three girls."

Claire snapped a photo with her phone and shook her head. "I can't argue with that. You're pretty lucky—but so are they."

With her husband and two daughters gathered around her, Wynn knew she was a part of an amazing family. She remembered the night she'd come to visit Claire and Joe when their baby was born. That night, she'd felt so alone and wondered if she would ever have a family of her own.

Penny liked to say she'd found her forever family. Wynn knew she'd found hers, too. They might not have become a family in the traditional way, but they were a family who loved each other enough to choose that love every single day.

* * * * *

*If you loved this story,
pick up the other books
in the* FAMILY BLESSINGS *series,*
THE DAD NEXT DOOR
A BABY FOR THE DOCTOR
from author Stephanie Dees

Available now from Love Inspired!

*Find more great reads at
www.LoveInspired.com*

Dear Reader,

I knew Wynn was a larger-than-life character when she first appeared in *A Baby for the Doctor*. She's a world-changer with big dreams…and she'd made a big mistake. She needed a hero who could show her that even big mistakes can be redeemed by the God of restoration! Thankfully Latham (and his grandpa) were up for the job!

I hope you've enjoyed your time in Red Hill Springs as much as I have. I love hearing from readers! If you'd like to connect, you can contact me via my website at www.stephaniedees.com or facebook at www.facebook.com/authorstephaniedees.

Stephanie

Get 2 Free Books,
Plus 2 Free Gifts—
just for trying the
Reader Service!

Get 2 Free Books,
Plus 2 Free Gifts —
just for trying the *Reader Service!*

HOME *on the* RANCH

HRCBPA18

READERSERVICE.COM

Manage your account online!

- Review your order history
- Manage your payments
- Update your address

> *We've designed the*
> *Reader Service website*
> *just for you.*

Enjoy all the features!

- Discover new series available to you, and read excerpts from any series.
- Respond to mailings and special monthly offers.
- Browse the Bonus Bucks catalog and online-only exculsives.
- Share your feedback.

Visit us at:

ReaderService.com